Crossover

Mel Andrews

Copyright © 2021 Mel Andrews
All rights reserved
First Edition

Fulton Books, Inc.
Meadville, PA

Published by Fulton Books 2021

ISBN 978-1-64952-274-0 (paperback)
ISBN 978-1-64952-275-7 (digital)

Printed in the United States of America

I want to dedicate this book to the people who believed I could actually write a book, my husband, my daughter, my son, and my sister. A special thank you to my "Megan" who went through this entire process with me and never let me quit. Love you.

M-

Prologue

ABBY KNOWS SHE will die young. She can remember being a child and telling her mom this profound statement to which she will give her ever-familiar "uh-huh." Some people just know, and she is one of those people.

Before her ever fateful day, she lives her best life. She has three, yes three, husbands in her lifetime (not her proudest moment) and two beautiful children. Her daughter, Megan, just turned twenty-seven, and her son, Brody, just turned twenty-one. Megan just had baby number three. Her grandkids are her pride and joy. She has the time of her life with them. Abby has had her challenges in life, but she welcomes them because she has a strong faith in God. God knows exactly what he is doing. Her life is not perfect, but it is hers, and she embraces every bit of it.

Even though she has two great kids, as with any family, they have their problems. Her kids rarely interact as adults, and if they do, it ends with arguments. With husband number one, she has Megan. With husband number two, she has Brody. Neither father has anything to do with their own children, and husband number three tries his best to make up for their neglect. Life is definitely not perfect.

Let's fast-forward to husband three, Ben. They are happily married, and he is the love of her life. Abby finally gets it right. They have had their moments of doom like any marriage, and they always work things out. Raising children that are not his own can definitely take a toll on a marriage. As the kids get older, things get much easier for them. They have their date nights, travel as much as they can, and spend lots of their time with the grandkids.

Her daughter, Megan, is her best friend. They confide in one another. Megan is her rock. After all, she gives Abby three of the most important little people in her life.

Now, Brody, he is her soul mate. Their souls connect on another level the day he is born. He has also been her biggest challenge. He tries to push her away, but she is there, always there.

Let's get to the ever-fateful day. Abby remembers driving on her way to pick up the grandkids—Jackson, who is four; Maddie, who is two; and Romy, who is seven months old. She is blessed to have two days a week with them all to herself. Driving on the interstate almost to her destination, out of nowhere, a car hits her head-on, killing her instantly, finding out later that it was a drunk driver. However, she cannot leave and will not leave this earth or her family.

THE DAY ABBY died starts out like any other day. She and Ben have their routines. Their life is comfortable, and she loves that she can count on the familiarity of it all.

"Good morning, beautiful," Ben says.

Hearing Ben say this every day never gets old to Abby.

"Good morning, darlin'," Abby says, bending over to kiss the top of his head.

He is already up and about. One of the many things Abby loves about him is that he is always busy. He is semiretired, telling Abby that if he fully retired, she may as well put him in the ground. She laughs every time he says that.

"What are your plans today, Mr. Stevens?" Abby says as she pours herself a cup of coffee.

"I am going to finish the yard work today. I have been so busy I haven't had time to get it finished. What are you and the kids going to get into today?" Ben says.

"I promised Jackson and Maddie we would go to the park today and take a picnic lunch. I was thinking for dinner, let's grill some burgers, and I will make a yummy salad," Abby says.

"Sounds perfect to me. I better get out there and get this done before it gets too hot. Have a fun day with the kids. Love you," Ben says.

"Love you more," Abby says.

Abby loves to watch the kids and spend time with them. She is at a point in her life where she is just starting to relax and enjoy her life. She has always worked so hard most of her life. Until she meets Ben, she is on her own taking care of her two children. Megan is ten and Brody four when they meet. Having two children doesn't scare him away. He loves Abby and thinks she is worth every challenge that comes with it.

Abby is a veterinarian and just last year retires from the practice. She does that for twenty-six years. She turned fifty last year, so she decides that she and Ben should enjoy their lives a little bit more as he is twenty years her senior. They have made plans to travel to each state, and after that, they will visit different countries. Right now, she is enjoying being with the kids. They are only little once she will tell Ben.

Abby grows up in a family with four older sisters. She is the baby. Normally, the baby is spoiled, but not in this case. Abby has a rough childhood, no doubt making her the loving, caring mother and grandmother she is today. She, without a doubt, loves her parents and respects them, but she is never sure they feel that for her. Out of the four sisters she has, she only clicks with one of them. Those two grow up taking care of each other. Abby loves her sister Hazel, seven years her senior, but in their hearts, they are identical twins. They now live in different states but have remained close to one another. Thank goodness for cell phones. They have become pros at texting and sending pictures.

After everything Abby has been through in her life, she now feels like her life is in a good place. This is giving her a calm she has never felt. As Abby sits in her office thinking about the surprise she has for Ben tonight, she can't help but smile. She has made reservations for a cruise leaving in three weeks for their anniversary. He will be so surprised as she never plans a vacation. That has always been his job. She places the folder she will give Ben tonight in her top drawer.

"One Abby, zero Ben," Abby says out loud as she smiles.

Abby waves at Ben in the yard as she pulls out of the driveway, heading out to pick the kids up for their day of sun and fun. She pulls onto the interstate, listening to her favorite song, thinking about the day she will have with the kids, and the car comes out of nowhere going at a rate of speed Abby can never avoid even if she would have seen him in time. The car slams into Abby's, and in an instant, she is gone.

"What is going on?"

Abby sees her lifeless body in her car. People are everywhere trying to save her.

Come on, Abby. You can do this, she says to herself.

Nothing, there is nothing. They are trying desperately to save her. They announce her dead on the way to the hospital. She never has a chance. Abby is sitting beside her body, not knowing why she is still there or what she should do now. She is numb and in a daze. They have called her family, finding her cell phone in her purse.

Abby says, "God, I don't understand what is going on here? I am a believer, a firm believer of you and Heaven. You can't keep me here. I can't watch my family grieve."

She sits and just stares at herself. She can't stop staring. She is so angry.

"What is going on?" she screams.

No one hears her. She cries and cries so hard. She lies with her head on the gurney where her lifeless body now lays. She can't move and won't move. Everything is running through her head. It is like a blur. She sees all of her past life running its course at a high rate of speed.

She thinks, *This is it. I am seeing all of this on my way to Heaven.*

Abby hears a door open, and she opens her eyes, and in walks a doctor with Ben, Megan, and Brody.

Megan screams, "No, no, no!" And she falls to the floor on her knees. Looking at the doctor, she says, "Can't you do something? Do something!"

The doctor quietly tells them again that Abby has died instantly. There is not one thing anyone can do to save her. Ben, Brody, and Megan cry, cry like Abby has never seen before. Brody clings to Ben like his life depends on it. Abby sits staring at them. She is so numb. Her body won't move. Over an hour passes, and they are still there with Abby's body. Ben says he will make arrangements to have Abby cremated. Megan and Brody say they will help him with the celebration of life. They are all shells of what they once were before this fateful day.

The next day, Abby is still in the hospital room where her body once was. She is confused, not knowing why she is still there.

What am I supposed to do? she says to herself.

For some reason, she knows that if she wants people to see her, she can make that happen. She doesn't know how she knows this, but she just does.

Abby thinks to herself, *Who would I show myself to? My family is clearly going through enough without me showing up. Hi, there. Its' me your wife, your mom.*

She laughs out loud. She laughs. She laughs harder than she ever has. The irony of what is happening to her doesn't go unnoticed. She has, in fact, predicted this early demise. She isn't ready. She has too much left to do with her family.

Abby's family has a beautiful celebration of life for her. Their grief is overwhelming. She just wants to take all their pain away. Nobody ever gets a front row seat to all the pain that death leaves behind. As Abby is there looking at her friends and family, she realizes her anger. She is so pissed off why did this have to happen and why now. She has a new grandbaby that will not know her nana loves her more than the air she breathes. She will not see her son get married and have kids of his own. She will not be there to take care of her husband as he ages. This is all so unfair, and she cries. She cries so hard because she just wants to be with her family. She has so much more life to live.

To stand there looking at her family and seeing their sadness, it is just heartbreaking. She wants to scream "I am still here, right here," but she just stands there frozen in time. She is sitting right beside her daughter who has spent the night before consoling her four-year-old grandson. Abby and Jackson are two peas in a pod. They are so close and always going on adventures together. She looks over at her son. His sadness is deep. He has not spoken a word to anyone. She is not sure where his head is at this point, but she knows it is not in a good place.

Abby's sister Hazel is there with her entire family. She looks devastated. She has been so good to Ben and the kids, helping them through all this. Her husband on the outside is a trooper. He is being a gracious host during this celebration. What he doesn't know is she has seen him take those shots of bourbon.

Hazel is there with her family. She has been a rock. She has always been there anytime they have needed her, and this is no exception. She has kept a close eye on Megan and Brody, looking after them like they are her own. Abby and Hazel have been busy with their own families and have not visited each other as much as they should.

Now as Hazel sits and listens to all the wonderful things people have said about her sister, she thinks, *Why did we wait to go on that vacation? Why did we put off our visits?*

Now, it is too late. She will never see Abby again. As Abby looks at her family, she wonders what will happen to them now. She is the one who brings them altogether. Without her, will they have any kind of relationship at all? Maybe that's why she is still here to make sure that gets done. Abby has not shown herself to anyone yet, not yet.

Megan

"HURRY UP! WE are going to be late, Jax!" Megan says.

"Mom, where are my shoes?" Jackson yells down the stairs.

Megan rolls her eyes, thinking how many times does she need to tell him where his shoes are when they always keep their shoes in the same place every day.

"They are in the closet downstairs," she says.

Taking all the kids to day care every day instead of them being with Abby has taken a toll on Megan. Losing her best friend and her mother has also taken a toll. She cries herself to sleep every night and puts on a brave, smiling face for her kids and her husband, Cam, in the morning. Watching Jax put his shoes on, her phone rings, and she notices it is Ben *again*. He has called nonstop since the celebration of life.

"Mom, are you going to answer that?" Jackson says.

"Oh no, it's a wrong number," Megan says.

She loves Ben. It is not that she doesn't. She just can't bear to hear his sad voice right now. She does not have the energy to try and lift him up too. Ben has been a great stepdad to her and Brody, a good provider, and loving in his own way. He does the best he can, thrown into a family with two kids who are not his own. She and Brody spend most of their childhood trying to piss Ben off just to see if he will leave too. Ben sticks around, and now, all he wants is to make sure they are all right. Megan gets the kids dropped off and gets to work a little late. She is the boss so she gives herself a pass. She has had her own successful photography business for three years now. She is the best in her industry. It is her passion, and she loves what she does. Her phone dings, and her heart skips a beat. For a second, she expects it to be her mom. They would always text back and forth throughout the day. She sadly looks at her phone, and it's Cam asking her to pick up some milk after work and that he will be late.

Sure, Cam, I do it all, she says to herself.

Since her mother's death, she has been on edge, and everything seems to get to her. She wonders if this is her new normal.

She has not spoken to Brody since the celebration of life. She sits wondering how he is doing and decides to give him a call. He answers on the third ring.

"Hello," Brody says.

"Hi, Brods, how's everything going? Are you doing okay?" Megan says.

"Hey, Meg, I'm hangin' in there. How about you?" he says.

"Same, hangin' in there. Just wanted to check in and see if you needed anything or maybe wanted to stop over for dinner this weekend?" she says.

"Sounds good. Just text me, and let me know the day and time. Thanks, Meg," he says.

"Okay. Love you, Brods," she says.

"Love you too, Meg. Bye," he says.

His voice is sad, and Megan knows that he misses their mom as much as she does. She knows she can't fix any of their sadness, but she just wants the feeling to end. Sometimes, it seems too much to handle. She goes through each day the same she always has, but there is no joy, no passion, and not an ounce of laughter. She and Abby have a relationship most daughters would be jealous of. They laugh until their tummies hurt, they cry at movies, and they love to talk about the kids. Now, she feels lost. There is a hole where her joy used to be.

A knock on her office door startles her back to reality.

"Come in," she says.

In walks her office manager, Helen.

"Good morning, Helen. What's up?" Megan says.

"Meg, I just wanted to say again how sorry I am about Abby, and if you need anything at all, help with the kids or errands to run, please let me know. I am here for you whatever you may need," Helen says.

Megan swallows hard, trying to hold back the tears.

"Thank you, Helen. That means so much to me," Megan says.

Her mom is the nicest person on the planet. Anyone who knows Abby loves her. She is the most giving person Megan has ever known.

Ugh, Mom, I can't do this life without you, Megan says to herself.

Little does she know Abby hears every word and is right there with her.

At the end of the day, Megan picks up the kids and got the milk, and they head home. Dinner, baths, books, hugs, kisses, and they are all finally in their beds. Megan sits alone in her kitchen with her glass of wine. She has never been much of a drinker. That is until Abby is gone. Now, this is her normal. This makes her, for just a little while, feel a little bit better. Cam walks in.

"I will take a glass of that. How was your day, honey?" he says as he gives Megan a kiss on the top of her head.

"It was good, same ole same ole," Megan says.

She knows how much Cam loves her and has been worried about her, yet she does not want to talk to him, not right now. She just wants to be alone with her thoughts.

"I am going to get a bath. I saved dinner for you. It is in the refrigerator. Love you," Megan says.

"Love you too, Megs. I'll be up in a while," Cam says.

She needs to get out of there before she starts to cry. She never wants them to see her cry. She is the strong one, the one who holds her family together. After her bath, she heads to bed and, once again, cries herself to sleep.

Brody

THE ALARM CLOCK buzzes and buzzes. It takes Brody a second to realize what the noise is. He quickly presses snooze, rolling over to catch some more sleep. Sleep has never been a big thing for him, but since Abby passed away, that's all he wants to do. Three months before she died, he finally gets his own place. He and Abby go shopping for everything he will need to be on his own. It is a milestone for him and Abby. He is stoked to finally have his own place. He is a hard teenager to deal with, getting in some trouble with drugs and alcohol. The last couple of years, he has really grown up, taking his life much more serious. During the troubled times, he and Megan grew apart, and since Abby has been gone, he now realizes how much he needs her.

  He gets up after the next buzz of his alarm, getting his shower and getting ready for work. He has been through the jobs in the past, trying to figure out what his passion is. He fell into a nonprofit that helps animals and the community. After a year and a half, he now runs the place. He found his best friend at this shelter, Bogo, who someone left in a dumpster when he was born. Brody takes him home as soon as he is able to be adopted, and now, Bogo goes everywhere with him. He is lucky to have a job where he can take his dog.

  Brody sits in his office going over upcoming meetings, and he just can't seem to focus. It is 9:00 a.m., and Abby would have called him by now. She always checks in with him and Megan several times a day. Sometimes, he would just send her to voice mail what he wouldn't give for her to call him right now. After Megan calls him yesterday, inviting him to dinner, he realizes just how much he needs his sister in his life. She has always looked out for him. It seems like it has always been them against the world.

Abby and Megan's relationship has always made Brody a little jealous. It is the kind of relationship he wants with his dad. He never gets that. All his dad gives him is emotional trauma, and he decides long ago to cut him out of his life completely. He has Ben for a dad although it is not the same. Ben has always been there and is good to him.

Abby always tells him to be a present uncle to Megan's kids. He is always too busy or too high to care about that. Losing Abby has made him think about being there for his family. He vows at her celebration of life to be more present and to make sure they are all going to be all right.

It's like you are right here with me, Mom, he says to himself.

She is there, right there.

Brody always goes out with friends at night, but the mere thought of that makes him anxious. Abby is his rock, his go-to person when anything is going on in his life. She has been his and Megan's constant, the one they can always count on no matter what the circumstance. He wants to hear her voice and see her face. He is so damn mad at the person who took her away. His emotions are high, going from sadness to anger. He puts on a brave face at work and around others, but inside, he is a mess. He takes out his phone. He has a saved voice-mail message from Abby that she left a while back. He presses Play.

"Brods, it's Mom. I am making your favorite tonight so I will see you and Bogo for dinner. Love you, darlin'. Hope your day is going great. See you tonight."

He sits and listens to that over and over with tears streaming down his face. He looks forward to Saturday night with Megan and the kids. He hopes Ben will be there too. He just wants to be surrounded by all of them. He knows they need him as much as he needs each one of them.

Ben

THE DAYS AFTER Abby's celebration of life seem to go by like a blur to Ben. He sits in the kitchen on a sunny morning just staring out the window, watching their two dogs lay in the sunshine. Abby loves those dogs like they are her kids, and now, they even have a sadness about them. Some days it is even hard to get out of bed. Where will he fit in now? What will he do? Will the kids have anything to do with him? Will he get to see the grandkids? These are all questions that have been playing in his head for days. He loves the kids. He loves them like they are his own. Abby is always the one who organizes family events. She keeps them all together. Now, who will do that?

Ben has some good friends that have really helped him out the last few days, calling and bringing food over. Some even offer to help with the house.

"I always thought I would go first, Abbs," he says out loud.

Now, he wonders just what he will do without her. He has slept on the couch ever since her death. The thought of sleeping in their bed without her is more than he can bear. Ben has always been Mr. Funny guy, always a good joke to tell. He has learned from an early age to use humor as a way to deflect his pain. He never knows his father as he died before Ben is born. It is always just him and his mom. He thinks it is his job to make her happy and to make her smile. Now, as an adult, he still feels the need to make everyone around him happy. He loves to hear Abby laugh and loves to see her smile. He always tells her that it is her smile that makes him fall in love with her.

The phone rings, and it startles him back to reality.

"Hello," he says.

"Hi, Ben. I am so sorry it has taken me so long to return your calls," Megan says.

"Kiddo, don't ever be sorry for needing time to yourself. I am the one who is sorry for being such a pest. I just wanted to make sure you were doing okay and to let you know I am here for you and the kids," Ben says.

"Are you doing okay?" Megan asks.

"I miss her so much, Megs, as I know you do. The house seems so big and lonely without her. It will just take time. We need to give ourselves time," Ben says.

"You are right. It will take time, but we are here for you, Ben. This family loves you very much," Megan says.

"I know you do, and I love all of you too," he says.

"I was calling to see if you would come over for dinner on Saturday. Brody is coming over, and the kids miss you. We would all love to spend time with you," Megan says.

"Count on it. I will be there. Love you, kid," Ben says.

"Love you too, Ben. See you Saturday," Megan hangs up.

Ben loves those kids like they are his own. Megan and Brody will always be taken care of by him. Nothing will ever change that. It seems like yesterday that he meets the two of them. They are broken, broken from the damage their so-called fathers do to them. Abby always says getting someone pregnant does not make you a father. How true in this case. It takes the kids a long time to trust Ben. He now knows they are meant to be in his life. They will get through this together. He will make sure of it.

After the call, Ben picks up a picture of him and Abby. It is the last time they go skiing. She looks so happy. They aren't always happy together. Life brings pain and happiness. They weather it all. Their love always gets them through the hard times.

Replaying the last time he saw her in his head is all he seems to do lately. She looked so beautiful when she left that morning. She was always beautiful to him. She never liked to be complimented, but that did not stop him from telling her every chance he got. He said, "I love you," and she said, "Love you more." Those were her last words to him. They had plans, plans for the weekend, plans for the holidays, plans for vacations.

His anger gets the best of him, and he screams, "Fuckkkkkkk! Why in the hell would she die and that drunk live? Why? Where is the logic in that?"

As he thinks this, he knows he will never get over God doing this to her, to him, and their family.

He sits down in her office looking for any bills she has that might need to be paid. He feels like he is invading her privacy. He opens the top drawer of her desk and pulls out a folder, not sure of what it is. He opens it and starts to cry. His heart feels like it is literally breaking in half. He is floored that Abby was going to surprise him with this trip. She never plans trips. That is always Ben's doing. She is the kindest person he has ever known and will ever know. Abby has spent her entire life making others happy and secure. He sits staring at their picture on her desk. He doesn't know how he will make it without her.

Hazel

HAZEL IS ABBY'S sister, her best girlfriend in life. The two of them had a rough childhood, growing up very poor and living in the worst neighborhoods. They make it a point to always take care of each other. A day doesn't go by without the two of them talking or texting. They try their best to stay close after Abby moves to another state. The move is hard and takes a couple of years for the both of them to adjust.

Hazel and Abby talk about everything. There is not one thing off-limits. The only thing Hazel ever left out of their conversations is the fact that she has been battling an anxiety issue for a few years now. She is off and on with her medication. She has good days and bad days, mostly bad days. She has hidden this from Abby because Abby worries way too much for the people she loves, and Hazel does not want to add to her list of things.

Hazel has always been the funny one. She is the one who makes people laugh especially in times that are scary or sad. She and Abby together could have had their own comedy show. Everyone loves to be around the both of them. They have good energy together. Their souls are definitely on another level.

Hazel has three children, two girls and a boy. They are all grown with kids of their own. She has been married for over thirty years to a wonderful man, John. She and John are meant to be, and he is a part of their family from the get-go. Abby loves her brother-in-law like a brother she never had. John and Abby are golf buddies. Anytime they all get together, there is golfing involved. They accept Ben from the start, and he and John become fast friends. The four of them vacation together whenever they could make the time.

Hazel hasn't worked outside the home in many years. She always says she is a princess, and John treats her just like one. Before she decides to stay home and raise the kids, she is a nurse for a local hospital. Her kindness and patience make her the best in her field.

After the celebration of life for Abby, Hazel tells Megan and Brody she will be there for them no matter what they need. She means that and has every intention to make a visit soon. She will probably stay longer than they want her to, but she really doesn't care. She needs them as much as they need her.

Her anxiety is much worse since Abby's accident. She has been to see her doctor, and he has increased her medication. Most days, she feels like a zombie and has tried to pretend Abby is still alive. She also knows this is not a healthy way to think.

Hazel calls Megan, Brody, and Ben regularly. They all say they are doing fine and staying busy. She knows this is a lie because she tells her husband and kids the same thing every day. She knows it will take time to feel less pain. There will always be a void in Hazel's heart, an emptiness, and she knows one day they will be together again.

Abby and Ben

DAYS GO BY, and all Abby can do is watch her family. She wants them to see her, but she just watches.

Ben is sad, no doubt, but he is being so strong for the kids. He puts on a brave face for them and gives them his time and love. Abby always thinks he will be fine without her, but seeing him now, she is not so sure. He seems so lost. Abby has never seen this kind of sadness in him. She wants to hug him so tight and tell him she is there for him. She doesn't know how long she will be here or why she is still here. She can't bear for them to lose her twice. Why is her life over? Why does she have to leave her precious family? Why? These are things she intends to find out.

Abby is sitting in her kitchen looking out the window at the beautiful blue sky in a daze. She doesn't hear Ben come in. He opens the refrigerator, and the noise startles Abby. She turns around and sees him standing there. She just wants to hug him, hug him, and never let him go. He stands there looking inside for what seems like an eternity and then closes it without getting anything out. Abby thinks he has lost weight. She is sure he is not eating much. He looks so sad as he wanders around the kitchen looking for something and nothing at all.

Ben is standing at the sink looking out the window, and Abby knows she has to touch him. She wants to feel his arms around her. She walks up behind him and touches his back. Ben quickly turns around and sees nothing. He sits in the chair and starts to cry. Abby knows now she has to show herself to him, and the two of them can figure out how to get her to cross over.

"Ben," Abby says behind him.

He gets up and turns around, seeing Abby standing there. Ben closes his eyes tight.

No, no, Ben. You are not seeing this. You are tired. You are sad. She is not here, he says out loud to himself.

He opens his eyes, and Abby is still standing there in front of him.

"Ben, I am here. I don't know why or how, but I am. I have seen everything from the hospital to the celebration of life. We have to figure this out. Why am I here, and what should I do now? Please help me, Ben," Abby says.

Ben just stands there looking at her. He reaches out his hand and touches her face, feeling her soft skin on his hand. He grabs her and hugs her.

"I am losing my mind," Ben says.

"I know. That's how I feel, Ben, but I am still here. We have to figure this out," Abby says.

They stand there hugging each other for what seems like hours.

They sit at the kitchen table, and all Ben can do is stare at her. Is she real? Is this really happening? Ben knows he hasn't slept much since Abby died. Maybe his mind is playing tricks on him. Maybe this is all wishful thinking. Maybe he is having a dream. He closes his eyes and focuses on his breathing, slowing down his heart rate. As he opens his eyes, Abby is still there.

"Ben, I know this is a lot to handle. I am having a hard time with it too, but please know this is real, and I am in front of you," Abby says.

Real or not, Ben decides to go with it and see where this thing goes.

"Do the kids know about this?" Ben says.

"I have not shown myself to them. I wanted to figure this out first. I am not sure they can handle losing me twice," Abby says.

"Oh, but you think this is something I can handle?" Ben says angrily.

Abby just looks at him and doesn't know if showing herself to him is a good idea. She should have just figured this out on her own and left him alone, but he is her partner. Through bad times and good, that is what they promised each other.

"I'm sorry, Abbs. I am so sorry I snapped at you. We will figure this out together," Ben says.

Abby is sure that there is nobody else that can help her figure this out.

Abby and Ben spend the rest of the day talking about all the things they wish they could have done together. They always think they have time. Ben knows this won't last, but he feels like he can breathe again.

"Ben, get some rest. I will be here in the morning, and we can decide what to do about all of this. I love you so much, and I am sorry for the pain this has caused you," Abby says.

"I love you more, Abbs. We will figure it out," Ben says as he closes his eyes.

The next morning, Ben opens his eyes and looks at the clock.

"Nine forty-seven, really?" Ben says out loud.

He has always been an early riser, so this is nuts for him to have slept this long. He gets up and looks around. He does not see Abby anywhere. Was this a dream? He looks all through the house and nothing. He hears the dogs out back and thinks he forgot to bring them in last night. He really is losing it. He opens the sliding glass door to the backyard, and there they are playing with Abby. It is real. He isn't dreaming. She turns around, and he meets her outside.

"Good morning, sleepyhead," Abby says as she kisses his lips.

"Good morning, beautiful. Sure is good to see you," Ben says.

His heart feels lighter. He is just so happy to have her back. He knows this will not last so he intends to make the most of her being here.

Abby has been thinking all night about what to do about this. She knows that she has been left here to do something, and when that something is done, she will cross over. Now, trying to figure out what that something is, well that's another story. They are sitting in the sunroom, drinking their coffee, and Abby tells him her theory of having something left to do. He agrees with her but has no idea how they are going to figure this out. Ben tells her he is going to Megan's for dinner Saturday night, and Abby tells him she is going with him. She misses all of them so much. Ben doesn't think it a good idea for her to show herself to them, but he also knows Abby is a very determined woman.

They spend the day outside, enjoying the warm sun on their bodies. They have so much to talk about. Ben wants to know how it feels for Abby to go through what she does. She tells him everything, starting with how scared she was to see that car come out of nowhere. Since then, they have been informed that the driver has been incarcerated. The man who killed Abby will be in prison for many years. That does not bring her back. That does not take away any of the pain he has caused. Abby wants Ben to forgive this man. She feels if he holds on to the hate, it will just hurt him.

Ben just sits and looks at her, thinking of all the silly arguments they have had over the years. He wishes he could change all that and appreciate everything he has when he has it.

"Abbs, I have an idea. I found the folder in your desk with the surprise trip. This will sound crazy, but let's go. Let's go on the trip together. I know I will be the only one to see you, and I don't care. Let's go," Ben says with a smile on his face.

"Ben, we can't go touring the world when I need to find out why I am still here. I am not supposed to be here. I don't feel right. This all just doesn't feel right," Abby says sadly.

Ben knows she is right, and he feels selfish to want her to stay. How many people get their loved one back, even for just a little while? He just wants to make the most of her time here.

The Dinner

SATURDAY IS HERE. This is the day they are going to let the kids know she is here. Abby hasn't told Ben that she has seen them every day since her accident. She just wants to make sure they are doing okay. What is she thinking? Of course, they are not okay. Only time can heal their sadness. It is all still too fresh, and Abby is a huge part of their everyday lives. Megan stays extremely busy with work, Cam, and the kids. That seems to help her mind stay occupied. Brody has been worrying Abby the most. He seems off, not just sad, like there is something else going on with him. He has not been eating much and has lost weight. Abby has noticed when she is with him that he takes a lot of medicine for headaches. She wonders if the stress of all the sadness is causing him physical problems. When the kids finally see her, she wants to talk to Brody about what is going on with him.

Ben tells Abby that he needs to stop at the store before they head over to Megan's. He is in charge of bringing the wine. They get to the store, and Ben asks her to come in with him as Abby always knows which wine is the best. In the store, Abby is showing Ben the wines that are the best and what they go with. Neither one of them notice that several people are looking at Ben. They don't see Abby, so Ben looks like he is talking and laughing with himself. Ben has never been a person who ever cared what other people think of him. This trait will definitely come in handy.

Ben and Abby get to Megan's right on time. They get to the door, and Jackson swings open the door.

"Grandpa!" he says as he leaps into Ben's arms.

"Hey, big guy. Boy, have I missed you!" Ben says.

"I have missed you too, Grandpa," Jackson says.

Seeing her sweet grandson, Abby starts to cry. Ben notices this, grabs Abby's hand, and gives it a squeeze. Cam and Megan come out from the kitchen.

"Hey, Ben," Meg says as she gives him a hug.

"Hi, sweetheart. Thank you for inviting me for dinner," Ben says.

"Of course, and you do not need to be invited to come over here, by the way," Megan says.

Megan goes back into the kitchen to finish up some things, while Cam and Ben sit in the living room playing with the kids. Abby goes in the kitchen to see Megan. She loves to just watch her. Abby is just so proud of who she is. She is a wonderful wife and mother. Abby feels lucky to have been her mother.

While they are in the kitchen, she hears Brody come in. He is talking to Ben and Cam. After a minute or so, he comes in the kitchen.

"Hey, Megs, need any help in here?" he says while he gives her a hug.

"Thanks, Brods, but I am just waiting for the lasagna to finish baking. How are you doing?" Megan says.

"Oh, pretty good," he says as he grabs a beer out of the refrigerator.

Abby just sits and watches the both of them together. They haven't been so close in the past, but it looks like that is behind them, and they really need each other right now.

They talk about their jobs, the kids, and how they are coping with the loss of their mother. Megan has always been a straight shooter. She will always tell you how she feels and is very open. Brody, on the other hand, is very reserved. He will tell you he's fine even if he is on fire. They set the table and get everything ready to go. Brody goes and tells everyone dinner is ready.

Abby tells Ben that she wants to show herself to them before dinner gets started. Ben lets her know that whatever she wants to do, he is behind her one hundred percent.

They all get to the dining room and start to get seated when Abby says, "Hi, everyone."

The only person who is looking at her is Ben.

"Hello, family?" Abby says, looking confused at Ben.

They can't hear or see her. She doesn't know what is going on.

Ben says, "I will be right back, guys. Quick bathroom run."

He leaves the dining room, and Abby follows.

"Ben, I don't understand what is going on. I am doing exactly what I did with you. If I want you to see me, I think it, and that has worked with you," Abby says.

"Abbs, I have no idea what is going on, and I definitely can't tell you how to make it work," Ben says, grabbing Abby's hand.

"Let's go in and try it again. Maybe I am just nervous," Abby says.

They head back into the dining room, and everyone is getting their food on their plates.

Abby screams, "Hello, it is me, your mom," and nothing. They cannot see or hear her. Ben is just standing there. He doesn't know what to do. Abby looks so distraught.

Megan makes Ben a plate, and he sits down not knowing what else to do. Abby just stands next to him, listening to all the conversations. Ben knows she is sad. She wants to be able to talk to the kids, hug, and kiss them. Abby doesn't understand why Ben can see her and not anyone else. Is he the reason she is still here? Does he need her for something? This is much harder than she ever anticipated it would be.

Abby notices that Brody hardly eats anything at all. She asks Ben if he notices anything is off with Brody.

"I haven't really noticed anything," Ben says, and everyone looks at him confused.

Ben realizes that he answers Abby out loud.

"I was just saying I haven't really noticed anything different with this wine. It is a new brand I thought we would try," Ben says.

"It's really good, Ben," Megan says.

Ben dodges that bullet. He loves the kids and loves being with them, but he really wants this night to end so he can talk to Abby about what is going on.

Brody is telling everyone about a new wing they are adding to the shelter for abused animals so they will have to hire several new people.

"What about the girl he had a crush on? Is she still there?" Abby says.

Ben looks at her and laughs.

"Always the matchmaker," Ben says.

Brody looks at him confused.

"Who is a matchmaker?" Brody asks.

Ben then realizes he is talking to Abby, and they have no idea.

"Oh, I was just thinking out loud," Ben says.

Megan looks over at Brody with a concerned look on her face. Brody knows exactly what she is thinking because he is thinking it too.

Throughout the dinner, Ben is talking with Abby, not realizing that the others think he is unstable.

Jackson asks Ben if he will stay and read him a bedtime story. Ben will never turn down that offer. Megan gets the kids upstairs for baths while the guys stay downstairs and watch the fight that is on pay-per-view. While she is bathing the girls, she wishes so desperately Abby is there. She misses her more and more every day. Abby is right there with her. She just wished Megan knew that. She tries all night to get them to see her.

Brody comes upstairs as Megan is putting the girls to bed. Ben is in Jackson's room, reading him a story.

"Meg, I'm going to go on home. Thank you for dinner. It was delicious," Brody says.

"You're welcome. I'm glad you came. Are you feeling all right?" Megan asks as she looks at him concerned.

"I'm fine. I've had some headaches that have been hard to get rid of. I'm sure it's stress and all the other stuff we have been through lately," Body says.

"I'm worried about Ben. Do you think he is doing okay? You noticed it too, right? He clearly was talking to himself throughout dinner," Megan says.

Brody looks at her concerned and says, "Yeah, I noticed, and I will keep in touch with him to make sure he is okay. Anyway, love you," Brody says.

"Love you too. I will call you tomorrow. Be careful going home," Megan says.

"You sound just like Mom," Brody says sadly.

When he leaves, Megan feels an emptiness inside like she needs him to stay around. She has been feeling so anxious lately. Having Brody and Ben there sure has helped. She hears Ben in Jackson's room reading him a story, and she smiles. Abby is lying next to Jackson in his bed. They are both listening to Ben's story, and she smiles every time Jackson laughs. Megan walks in.

"Okay, time for sleep. Give hugs and kisses," she says to Jackson.

"Love you, Grandpa. Thank you for my story," he says as he gives Ben a hug and kiss good night.

"Love you, buddy. Get good sleep now," Ben says.

Ben gets ready to leave, giving Megan and Cam a hug and thanking them for a great evening.

"Be careful going home. We all love you, Ben," Megan says.

"Thank you for your love. I have never taken it for granted, Meg, and I love all of you too," Ben says.

He and Abby head home. He knows she is sad by the way she is so quiet.

"Abbs, I am so sorry they couldn't see you. I know you needed them," Ben says.

"Ben, now we have to figure out why you are the only one that can see me. Honestly, I am worried about Brody. He tried to make small talk and be a part of the family, but could you tell something was wrong?" she says.

"I just thought he seemed sad, and that is understandable," Ben says.

Abby knows in her heart there is something else going on. She has to figure out what it is before she can focus on her crossing over.

Ben asks Abby how she gets from point A to point B. These are things he has been wondering about and decides to ask her. She tells him all she does is think about the place or the person, and she is there. He knows she wants to keep tabs on the kids until they figure out what is going on with her. Knowing she can see them at any given time, he brings up the trip one more time.

"Abby, thank you for surprising me with that trip. I know we can't go, but it was the best surprise, and I love you for that," Ben says.

Abby doesn't say anything to him. She knows she has spent most of their marriage putting him and their relationship on the back burner. She wishes they would have had more time together.

Hopeful Ben

ABBY SPENDS THE next morning thinking about her life and what it has meant. Did she do everything possible to be a kind and giving person? Did she help enough people? She spends a lot of time talking to her kids about Heaven and Jesus. Now, look at her stuck in a world where only Ben can see her. What good is this going to do? How in the world can she make a difference now? She prays long and hard, wanting God to give her a sign and send her in a direction of what needs to be done and how.

Ben comes in the sunroom where she is sitting with the dogs. She doesn't hear him come in, so he stands there looking at her. He loves her so much. He knows that when it is time for her to go, he still will not be ready. He feels so lucky that he has more time with Abby. When someone you love dies unexpectedly, it is so hard to get over. You never get to say goodbye or any of the other things that you should really say every day. He intends on letting her know each and every day she is here just what an impact she has had on his life. The kids may not be able to see her, but he can tell them that she is here. Anything that needs to be said between them, he will be the go-between. He hopes Abby goes for this plan of his.

"Good morning, beautiful," Ben says as he kisses the top of her head.

"Good morning to you," Abby says.

"Abbs, I've been thinking I know the kids can't see you, but I can let them know you are here, and anything that needs to be said, I will say it for you. What do you think?" Ben says.

"Yes, that's a really good idea, but before we do that, let's figure out why I am still here in the first place. I have been making lists of things that I didn't get finished. I never volunteered at the homeless shelter. I meant to and never did. I started the suicide prevention program, and it never got it off the ground. Maybe these are reasons I am still here," Abby says.

"Abbs, people die every day, and there are always things left to do or things we didn't get around to. That can't be the reason. Let's just go through each day as we always would, and it will come to you. God left you here for a reason. He will show you that reason. Keep your faith," Ben says.

Ben sits and watches Abby. Everything she has ever done has been kind and caring. He knows that she is here because someone in their family needs her more than ever. He is determined to find out who that is.

Hazel

BEN AND ABBY are sitting outside when the doorbell rings. He goes to check out who it is and opens the door, and it is Hazel.

"Hazel, what are you doing here? I mean it's great to see you, but what is the visit for?" Ben asks.

"Hi to you too, Ben." She laughs. "I am here to check on the family and see if anyone needs me to help out in any way. I thought you might want someone here to help go through Abby's things? Anyway, I'll be staying with you, so we can get into all of that later. It is just good to be here. I can really feel Abby's presence here, and that feels good," Hazel says as she walks in the house with her suitcase.

Abby sees and hears all this, and she chooses not to show herself until she talks to Ben. If the kids can't see her, chances are nobody will but Ben.

Hazel puts her things in the spare room. She sits on the bed and looks around. Abby still has a picture of the two of them on the nightstand. It feels so good to Hazel just to be in a place that is Abby's. Abby is standing in the room, looking at Hazel wanting to hug her so tight. She misses her big sister and would love her advice what exactly she is supposed to do with this situation.

Hazel goes downstairs into the kitchen and grabs a beer.

"Come on, Ben. Let's go outside and catch up. Tell me how you and the kids are really doing," Hazel says as she goes out to sit in the sun.

Abby looks at Ben and laughs. Hazel has always been the boss of every situation, and most of the time, Abby needs that. Abby asks Ben if she should try and show herself to Hazel, and they agree to do that. But first, Ben goes outside to see why Hazel is really there.

"To what do I owe this surprise visit?" Ben says to Hazel, walking outside.

"I needed to be here, Ben. I can't really explain it. I just needed to be with you and the kids for a while. John sends his love. He truly misses all of you," Hazel says.

Ben sits down next to her, and they spend the next hour talking about old times. Abby comes out and sits next to Ben, and she mouths the word *now*.

"Hazel, I need to tell you something, and it is going to sound crazy, but it is one hundred percent true," Ben says.

"You can tell me anything. What's up?" Hazel says, looking at Ben.

"Abby is here. I can see her, touch her, hear her. It's like she never left. The kids can't see her. We tried to show her to them at dinner on Saturday, and they could not see her. So far, I am the only one who can see her."

Hazel takes a big long sip of her beer, looks at him, and says, "Okay, I understand, and I have also been pretending Abby is still here. It has helped me get through this. Actually, one of the reasons I am here is to show my brain that she is indeed gone. I needed to be in her house and see her not here. You will get through this, Ben. We can help each other."

Ben looks at Abby, and she is standing in front of Hazel.

"Okay, Abbs, do your thing," Ben says.

Hazel rolls her eyes under her sunglasses and closes her eyes, thinking that being here may have been more than she can handle. Ben is worse than she thinks.

"Hazel," Abby says.

Hazel opens her eyes, and right in front of her stands Abby.

"What the hell, Abby?" she screams. "You were never dead? This was all a joke? I don't understand what is happening here," Hazel says.

"Haz, I am dead. I just haven't crossed over, and we have no idea why. Nobody can see me but you and Ben," Abby says.

Hazel starts to cry and stands up falling into Abby's arms. Ben and Abby spend the afternoon telling Hazel everything they know, which is not much. Abby tells her that she thinks something is wrong with Brody.

Ben is on the phone in Abby's office and comes out saying that Megan needs him to pick up the kids from day care and stay with them for an hour or so. He doesn't tell her Hazel is in town yet. He figures the sisters need some time to figure this thing out.

"I'll be back soon. Love you," he says to Abby as he gives her a kiss on the lips.

"Love you more," she says as she flashes him her biggest smile.

"I will call Megan and Brody later tonight to let them know I am in town," Hazel tells Ben before he leaves.

Abby is telling Hazel what she feels like still being here but not really here. Hazel wants to know if she has to eat or drink and does she need sleep. She has a lot of questions to be answered. Abby does not need sleep and does not need food or water. She just exists. Abby tells her that she feels something pulling her in two different directions, here on earth and something of the unknown. She knows she needs to figure out what God is keeping her here for.

Hazel knows seeing and talking to Abby again save her life. She knows now she has to live, actually live her life instead going through the motions in a haze. If Abby can go through this, then she can live a life to be proud of. She tells Abby everything about her anxiety issues. Since Abby's death, Hazel cuts herself off from her family. She doesn't want to interact with anyone or be with anyone. She is always trying to get out of her own head, and that is how she does it. Telling Abby all this, she vows to make her life better and to appreciate the fact that God still has a plan for her.

Hazel is going to lay down for a while, so Abby wants to check on the kids. She starts at Meg's house. She loves just watching the kids. She misses playtime with her grandbabies. Just seeing them and listening to their voices make her happy. She wishes that they could see her and talk to her. Why in the world can Ben and Hazel see her and not her own children? This whole thing is beyond real. How is she going to figure this out? Ben is here still babysitting, and he has no idea she is there, so she gets to sit and observe. She knows he will be there for all of them no matter what.

I finally picked a good one, Abby says to herself.

Now, to check on Brody, she goes to Brody's, and he is asleep on the couch. She just sits and stares at him. He looks pale, and he has definitely lost some weight. Abby knows he needs to get checked out. How will she pull that one off? She reaches out to touch his hair. He will always be her baby.

"Hi, sweet boy. Oh, I wish you knew I was here," Abby says with tears running down her cheeks.

She sits there for the longest time just looking at him. She doesn't want to leave. She prays that God will just give her some answers. What does he need her to do?

"Please let my children be okay. They have been through so much in their lives. It is time for some happiness," Abby says out loud.

He has been asleep for a while, so she decides to check on him again later.

Going back to her house, she finds a note on the counter from Hazel saying she went to the store. Abby decides to go and find her.

At the store, she sees Hazel looking over the produce, so she walks up behind her and says, "Those look good."

Hazel jumps and says, "Damn it, Abbs. You can't sneak up on me like that!"

People turn to look at Hazel, not seeing who she is talking to. Hazel doesn't notice any of that.

"Hazel, I just came from Brody's, and he has been asleep all afternoon. It just doesn't feel right," Abby says.

They both continue to walk through the store.

"Okay, I am going to head over there later and will talk to him about it," Hazel says.

She and Abby stop walking, and Hazel grabs her by the hands.

"Abbs, we will figure this out. I promise," Hazel says, not having a clue that the people around her are looking at her with concern.

Abby sees the stares and throws an apple to Hazel, then another, and another. The both of them are laughing so hard they can't breathe. This whole invisible thing can be fun.

Hazel and Brody

HAZEL AND ABBY decide to head over to Brody's after they leave the store. Hazel knocks on his door, and it seems like forever before he answers.

"Aunt Hazel, what are you doing here?" Brody says, confused.

"Happy to see you too, babe," Hazel says as she hugs him tight.

"I am happy to see you, but just wasn't expecting you. Come in. Tell me what brings you to town," Brody says.

"I just needed to be here to see all of you and spend some time with you. With Abby gone, it has just been hard, and I just needed to be here, you know?" Hazel says, looking around at his apartment.

Abby is telling Hazel that she needs to talk to him about not feeling well.

"Abbs, I know. I got this," Hazel says out loud.

Brody looks at her with a puzzled look.

"Oh, Brods, we have always been close right?" Hazel says.

"Yes, we have. Are you okay?" Brody says.

"I am fine, but I need to tell you something. Your mom is still here. I know that sounds crazy, but she is. She is trying to figure out the reason she has not made that crossover yet. So far, Ben and myself are the only ones who can see her. This is all bizarre, I know, but, Brods, its real," Hazel says.

Brody just sits and stares at her. Is she really saying all these things to him? He has had the worst headache lately. Maybe his head is playing tricks on him. He closes his eyes and just breathes. He needs a minute. Hazel looks at Abby and shrugs her shoulders.

"I know this is a lot to take in, Brods. Please talk to me," Hazel says.

He says nothing, still sitting there with his eyes closed.

"Brody, are you all right?" Hazel says, now looking very concerned.

"Aunt Hazel, what are you talking about? Did you really just say to me that Mom is still here? I don't understand," Brody says.

"Okay. Look, I have never bullshitted you, Brods. I am the one who is truthful to a fault. I mean, you may not like what I say to you, but I have not and never will lie to you. Abby has not, well how do I put this, crossed over yet. She is still here with us. She is right here, right now," Hazel says, looking and pointing at Abby.

Brody looks to where she is pointing, seeing nothing. He looks back at Hazel confused and not saying a word.

"Abby, this is not working," Hazel says.

"Okay, okay, I am the only one who knows Brody went to rehab. We decided to tell everyone including Ben that he was on a trip last May with his buddies when in fact he was in rehab," Abby says.

"Wait, what? Why in the hell wouldn't you guys tell me this? I love your family like my own. I would have been there to help," Hazel says upset.

"Hazel, really? Come on, this is not about you right now. Just tell him!" Abby says loudly.

Looking over at Brody, Hazel says, "Brods, Abby just told me that you were not on a trip with your friends last May. You were in rehab. You are the only two that knew this."

Brody sits there in shock. Abby goes over and touches his face, and he feels that. He touches his cheek and feels the warmth of her. He starts to cry, and Hazel kneels down in front of him, hugging him and will not let go.

"Why is this happening? Why can't I see Mom? How are we going to help her?"

Brody has all these questions for Hazel, and she doesn't have one single answer for him.

"We haven't said anything to Megan yet. We are here because Abbs thinks something is wrong with you, Brods, and you know your mom knows you better than anyone. What has been going on? Are you not feeling well?" Hazel says to him, looking him over.

"I have just had these awful headaches, but I think they are from stress. I just haven't been myself since Mom died," Brody says.

Abby asks Hazel to tell him to make an appointment with their family doctor. She does that, and he does exactly that, getting one the following day. Abby is sitting beside him and grabs his hands in hers. He looks at Hazel and asks her if Abby is touching his hands. He can feel the warmth of them. Hazel says yes, and he looks straight ahead and tells Abby he loves her so much, and he will do anything to help her make the transition to where she is meant to be. They spend the next two hours talking and laughing at old times. Hazel is their go-between, and she learns that there is a lot of their lives she doesn't know about.

"We have to get back home. Ben will be wondering where we are. Stop by the house after your appointment tomorrow so we know what is going on," Hazel says as she hugs him goodbye.

"Okay, I will. I love you both so much. See you tomorrow," Brody says.

Ben and Abby

THEY GET BACK to the house and find Ben asleep in the family room with the TV on.

"Looks like the kids wore him out," Hazel says to Abby.

"I am going to turn in myself. I'm beat. I know what you are going to say, Abbs. You want to go to Megan's tomorrow to tell her you are here," Hazel says.

Abby smiles and says, "You know me way too well. Love you. See you in the morning."

Abby gives her sister a big hug. Abby goes in and lies with Ben on the couch. Not knowing how much longer she will be here, she wants to be near him as much as she can. Lying there, she thinks about the kids and her life, and she knows she raised good kids who are now amazing adults. She is so proud of them and the values they have. They are kind, gentle, and smart, and both have a wonderful sense of humor. She has always been their constant, the one person they can always count on no matter what. They are a team.

Ben has been so great through this craziness. Abby wonders if he will be okay when she has to leave for good. She will make sure he is. He deserves so much happiness. He has always been the one who makes sure everybody else is taken care of. How many men take on the responsibility of children that are not their own? She lies there listening to his heartbeat and wishing that she could have stayed on this earth to live out their life together. They are lucky to find each other. Ben saves her life, no doubt, and with him, the kids learn that not all men are bad. When Ben makes a promise to the kids, he keeps it. He is someone they can always count on.

Ben wakes up when the sun comes through the window and looks around for Abby, and she is not there. He hasn't meant to fall asleep on the couch. He has been more tired than usual lately. All this uncertainty with Abby has been upsetting to him. He knows he has to help her find her way to where she is supposed to be, but he really wants her to stay. It's unrealistic, and he knows that, but honestly, all this is unrealistic. He lies there thinking about all the wonderful times they have had together, all the memories they've created. They are lucky to have had each other. He knows this and is so grateful. He doesn't notice Abby staring at him in the doorway.

"Good morning," she says as she walks in and gives him a kiss.

"Good morning to you, beautiful. How did yesterday go with Brody?"

Abby tells him how everything goes and that he is going to the doctor today. She also tells him that she and Hazel are going to Megan's later to let her know that she is still here.

"Do you want me to go with you? I just know our time together is coming to an end, and I want to be with you as much as possible," Ben says as he pulls Abby on his lap.

"Yes, I would love that, and I want you with me too," Abby says as she kisses him ever so softly. "Hazel took the dogs for a walk so we actually have time to be alone if you know what I mean," Abby says as she stands up and grabs his hand, leading him to their bedroom.

She is thinking one more time, *I just need one more time with him.*

Their love is special, a love that she has searched her entire life for. She wants to make sure he knows how much she loves him.

Abby and Hazel

WHEN HAZEL GETS back with the dogs, she notices Abby outside sitting by herself. She grabs a cup of coffee and heads outside.

"Any news from Brody yet?" Hazel says as she gives Abby a hug and sits down next to her.

"Not yet, but it is early. He said he would call you when he was done," Abby says.

"I called Megs while I was on my walk with the dogs and told her I would be over later. We will tell her about you when we are there. Where is Ben?" Hazel says.

"He is showering. He wants to go with us when we go to Megs, which is a great idea. He can occupy the kids while we talk to her," Abby says.

They sit in the morning sun, talking about their lives and what they wish they could have done together before Abby died. They always want to do a girls' trip, and that never got done because they think they have time.

"I don't know when I am leaving, Haz, and I want you to know a few things. You have always been my person, and you have always been there for me since day one of my life. When I had the kids, you were always there for them too. We both have been through so much, not only with our childhood and the trials that brought, but as adults, we have weathered some heavy shit. Through everything, the one constant thing has been you. Thank you for being there through it all, for all of the laughs we have had and the tears we have shed. Thank you for loving my children like they are your own. Thank you accepting Ben as one of us from the very beginning, and thank you for always loving me without conditions. God has truly blessed my life, and you are at the top of those blessings. When you are alive, you take things like that for granted, and I have never thanked you for all of the wonderful things you have ever done for me. Thank you. I love you with all of my heart and soul. Let that love see you through the rest of your life. I will always be a part of your life because our hearts have always been connected from the start. Anyway, I love you, Haz, and thank you," Abby says as she hugs Hazel with all of her might.

Hazel cries, and she doesn't think the tears will ever stop. This is the grieving she needs, and who, of all people, is helping her through it, her Abby. She knows at that moment that she will be okay. Life without Abby will be different, no doubt, but she knows she will be strong and make it through.

"You better get us an amazing house together in Heaven. We always said when we get to Heaven, we will be together forever. Since you are going first, pick us a good one," Hazel says.

They need this time together to heal. Hazel hopes this time with Abby will help Ben and the kids heal. For the first time since Abby's death, Hazel's smile is not forced. She just feels good. Ben hears their conversation and decides to get things done in the house to give them some more time. When he first meets Abby and is getting to know her, he can't believe how close she and Hazel are. Ben is an only child, but he still does not know of any siblings that are as close as the two of them. He loves that Abby has that. Hearing about their childhood a time or two, he is grateful they have each other to get them through.

It has been over two hours since Brody is supposed to be at his doctor's appointment, and Hazel decides to call and see if he is all right. It goes straight to voice mail.

"He has his phone off, Abbs. Let's give him more time. You know, doctors are always running behind, and he did say he would call when he was done," Hazel says.

Hazel decides to text Brody to let him know they will be at Megan's and to come over there when he is done. Hazel asks Abby if she wants to go through her things and take care of that task so Ben will not have to. Of course, she doesn't want to, but she knows that will be hard for Ben to do, and she has things she wants to give to the kids, so they decide to get started on it. How crazy is this that the deceased will be going through her own things to see what her family may want to keep. This whole scene should be a movie. Abby wants Brody to have her engagement ring. She is hopeful he will find someone wonderful, and she could wear it as it represents so much love to her. She has a necklace with a diamond pendant she loves to wear. It means a lot to her, and she wants Megan to have that so when she wears it, she will know Abby is always with her.

They are going through a lifetime of things. Many of the things will go to the kids, such as pictures and different mementos. Abby comes across a bracelet that Hazel bought for her when she was going through a rough time in her life. It is engraved with "You are strength, you are courage, you are loved." That bracelet gets her through a lot in her life, and she hands it to Hazel.

"It is your turn to wear this bracelet. This will get you through whenever you are missing me," Abby says as she clasps it onto Hazel's wrist.

Hazel looks at the bracelet and back at Abby with tears streaming down her cheeks.

"I will never take it off, Abbs. You are my person," Hazel says.

Ben comes in and tries to help them go through some things, but it is just too hard for him, so he leaves them with the task and is thankful they are doing that. Abby puts things in a box for him that she thinks he may want in the future. When he is ready, he can go through it, and she hopes it puts a smile on his face. Three hours later, they are done. They have lots of laughs and tears, but it is done, and Abby is grateful Ben and the kids do not have to do that.

Abby and Megan

THE THREE OF them decide to head over to Megan's, and it is not lost on any of them that Brody still has not called about his appointment yet. Megan is at the door, waiting for Hazel to get there. She is excited to see her aunt. Without Abby, she is the next best thing. She sees Ben's car and goes out to greet them.

Hazel gets out and runs over to hug her. They hug each other, not wanting to let go. It makes Megan feel so close to Abby just having Hazel there. They go into the house, and Hazel looks for the kids. Megan says they are upstairs playing so they could talk.

"Megan, let's sit down. There is something I want to tell you," Hazel says as they all sit in the kitchen.

"What's up, Aunt Hazel? Are you okay?" Megan says with concern.

"There is no way to say this to you without sounding crazy, so I am just going to say it. Your mom is here. Right here," Hazel says, pointing to Abby.

"She has not crossed over yet and is here. So far, only Ben and myself can see her. There is no explanation for this. We don't know why or how," Hazel says.

"Wait, what? I heard what you said, but I can't wrap my head around this," Megan says, looking at Ben.

"Honey, it's true. Your mom is here," Ben says, looking at her, sadly wishing she can see Abby too.

Abby walks over and touches her arm. Megan flinches, looking at Hazel.

"Yes, she just touched you," Hazel tells her.

Abby reaches out and hugs her, and Megan feels this and starts to cry.

"Mom, I feel you. Please don't stop hugging me. Please don't leave me again."

She just leans into Abby and cries. Ben and Hazel just sit there not knowing what else to do. They watch Abby hold her daughter, her best friend in the world. The two of them are clinging to the only thing they have left. Minutes go by, and Abby lets go. Megan gets up, looking at Hazel and Ben.

"Now what? Why is Mom here? What are we going to do?" Megan says.

"We don't know, Meg. That's why we wanted you to know. If we could help her figure this out, then she could go to where she is meant to be," Hazel says.

"No, I don't want her to leave. Maybe she is here because she never should have died. Did any of you think of that? I can't do this. Not right now. This all has been too much for me. Mom being gone, work, the kids, and I am worried about Brody and Ben all the time. It is all just too much. Now, you come in here to let me know that Mom is still here and could I help figure out why. Okay, let me squeeze that into my day," Megan screams.

She sits back down and puts her head on the table. She looks defeated, and the world has not been on her side lately.

Ben goes over and sits next to Megan, grabbing her hand. He smiles gently.

"I know things have been tough. I know how close you and your mom were. I know you need her. I know you want to see her and have her here with you. She is here with us for now. We don't have the answers on why. All of this is bizarre and frustrating. I just want you to know that I am here with you and for you. I am here for you, Meg. I always have been and always will be," Ben says.

For the first time in a long time, she smiles.

"I know. Thank you. This whole thing makes me feel like I am losing my mind. What are Mom's thoughts on why she is still here? Did she tell you anything?" Megan says.

"She has no idea, none whatsoever. She says she will focus on why after we find out what is going on with Brody," Ben says.

"I know it's awkward and weird, but Ben and I can be your go-between if you and your mom want to talk," Hazel says.

"Thanks for being here, Aunt Hazel. You never let us down," Megan says.

Hazel pulls out the necklace that she and Abby found in her things and hands it to Megan.

"Your mom and I went through her things, and she wants you to have this. It was very special to her," Hazel says as she looks at Abby.

"Tell her when she wears it to just know I am always with her and that I love her so much," Abby says.

Hazel looks over at Megan and tells her what Abby says. Megan puts the necklace on.

"Mom, I will never take it off. I need you with me every day of my life. I love you so much, and I am not sure I told you that enough when you were here. Thank you for being the best Mom a daughter could ever have. I will miss you every day of my life. This necklace will be the lifeline to all of the memories with you. Thank you," Megan says with tears running down her face.

Abby reaches over and wipes her tears. Megan can feel her on her skin, and she feels all of her mother's love. Hazel reaches into her purse and grabs a letter, handing it to Megan.

"There were letters in Abby's things, one to you, Brody, and Ben. Read that later. Abby said she wrote those a long time ago and still wanted you all to have them. Ben, yours is in the box of things that Abby put away for you," Hazel says.

Megan goes into her office to put the letter in her drawer.

Abby goes upstairs to watch the kids. She just sits and watches them. She loves the kids so much. They are a huge part of her life. When she thinks about that, she gets really angry at the fact that her life is cut short, and now they don't have her. They don't have their nana to grow up with and to make memories with. Where is the logic in this? What kind of God does this? Abby closes her eyes, and she knows deep in her heart that God did not do this to her. The fact is we live in a fallen world where bad things happen to good people every day. If you have been lucky enough to have learned about Heaven and God, well then you know life doesn't end when you die. It begins. Abby sits there watching these beautiful babies that she is blessed to hold and give her love to, knowing that she will figure this whole thing out and soon. Abby hears the commotion downstairs and knows Brody is here.

Brody and the Family

ABBY GOES DOWNSTAIRS to see what is going on, and she sees Brody. She can tell by the look on his face that he does not have good news. She walks over to him and hugs him. He knows that Abby is hugging him, and he just cries. He cries because he misses her, he cries because he has had the worst day, and he cries because life is really unfair. Megan goes over to hug him too.

"Brody, let's sit down. Tell us what is going on," Megan says.

"You know about Mom? You know she is still here?" he says to Megan.

"Yes, I know," Megan says sadly, sad for the both of them that are not able to see her.

Brody sits there looking at all of them. He can tell they are concerned about him, and he doesn't want to add to the pain they are already feeling.

"Brods, talk to us. What is it?" Hazel says.

Brody stands up to look at all of them.

"I have spent the day getting test after test done. I had an MRI and a CAT scan. They drew blood to check for different things. After all of that, they found a tumor in my brain. As luck would have it, there were two cancellations today, so they wanted me to go in and get a biopsy. They numbed the area on my head and did a needle biopsy. It was an all-day process. I won't know until tomorrow what they find. Not only the headaches, I have had some memory issues and sometimes trouble getting words out. I just thought all of this was because of the stress and sadness from Mom dying. I had no idea and honestly would not have went to the doctor if Aunt Hazel and Mom didn't come over yesterday," Brody says.

Abby runs to him and hugs him. She has tears streaming down her face.

"Tell him that we will get through this. He will be okay," Abby says to Ben and Hazel.

"Brods, your mom says you will get through this. You have all of us for support," Hazel says to him.

"Tell him he will be okay," Abby says.

"No, Abby, you don't know that," Hazel says to her out loud.

Megan and Brody just look at Hazel. She excuses herself and goes outside. Megan and Ben go over to hug him, to let him know that, as a family, they will get through this.

"Ben, I don't really want to be alone. Could I go get some of my things and Bogo to stay with you guys for a while?" Brody says, looking at Ben.

"Yes, of course!" Abby says, almost screaming.

Ben looks at her and then at Brody.

"Yes, absolutely. That's a great idea. You definitely do not need to be alone through any of this," Ben says.

"Love you, Megs. I am going to cut out of here and go get my things and head to Mom and Ben's. I am so tired, and they gave me some pain meds that I want to get started on," Brody says, hugging Megan bye.

"Love you, Brods. I will be over tomorrow to check on you and find out the plan for your recovery," Megan says.

"Brody, how about I go with you so you can go ahead and take the medicine. I will drive," Ben says.

"Thought you'd never offer, Ben."

Brody laughs as they head out the door. Hazel comes back in and sees Abby and Megan both crying.

"I leave you two for a minute, and you both fall apart," Hazel says.

They all laugh at that. All of them are emotional. The family has had its share of hard times, and their faith is really being tested now.

"Mom, I know you can see and hear me, so just know we are all in this together. The love our family has for each will get us through anything," Megan says out loud.

"Haz, tell Meg that she is the strongest person I know and that I love her so very much," Abby says.

Hazel tells her what Abby says, Megan reaches out her hand, and Abby grabs it and hugs her. The warmth Megan feels when her mother hugs makes her feel like she can get through anything.

"We better get home, Haz. I need to get a room ready for Brody before he gets there," Abby says.

Hazel stands up and reaches out to Megan for a hug.

"We will see you tomorrow, babe. Abby wants to get home and get things ready for Brody," Hazel says.

"Yes, see you tomorrow. I will come over to Mom and Ben's. Love you both," Megan says.

GETTING BACK HOME, Hazel and Abby get busy getting the room ready for Brody with fresh sheets and blankets on the bed and making sure his bathroom has everything he will need. As they are finishing up, Brody walks into the room.

"Thanks, Aunt Hazel and Mom, if you are in here. I am going to shower and go to sleep. It has been a rough day," Brody says as he lays his stuff down on the floor.

Abby grabs his hand and squeezes it. Brody looks down at his hand and smiles.

"I love you too, Mom," he says.

Hazel gives him a hug, and they leave him to rest.

Ben is in the kitchen having a drink when they walk in.

"Well, how did it go with Brody?" Hazel says.

"It's the same thing with Brody. He feels bad. He's sick because this family is dealing with so much from Abby's death and now return. I told him it is time to focus on himself. We would all be here for him," Ben says.

"One thing I have learned through all of this is we have no control over what happens to us. We can eat healthy, exercise, go to church, do all of the things we need to do in order to stay on track, but ultimately, we have zero control. I don't know when I will leave, and I don't know what will happen to Brody. All I know is right now," Abby says.

The three of them stay up late, talking about the past and the future. Laughter really is the best medicine. When they laugh, things seem right with the world.

Everyone is asleep, so Abby goes in to check on Brody. He is asleep. He looks peaceful. She just sits there staring at him, thinking of all the things that they have been through. He has come through the abuse his biological father dishes out, and he has overcome addiction. Abby worries about him taking pain medicine. She doesn't want him to relapse. All this is out of her control, so she prays. That is all she knows to do. She is still sitting there when the sun came up, and he is still asleep. She goes outside to feel the warmth of the sun on her skin. Ben sees her and comes out.

"Let me guess. You sat and looked at Brody all night, didn't you?" Ben says.

She laughs. "You know me too well. I need him to be all right, Ben," Abby says as she hugs him.

"Like you said, Abbs, it is out of our control. Try to stay positive," Ben says.

They hold each other, letting the sun soak through their skin.

Hazel and Brody come outside with their coffee.

"Hey, gang," Hazel says.

Abby looks at Brody and then Hazel.

"Ask him how he is feeling, Haz," Abby says.

"Yeah, I already asked him that. He says his head feels like it may explode. He just took more medicine. Hopefully, he will feel better soon," Hazel says.

"Mom, try not to worry. Even if we get the worst news ever, let's not let this bring us down," Brody says, looking at Ben.

He has no idea where to look for her. Abby reaches out and touches his arm, and he smiles.

"It is only eight o'clock. We should know something by ten o'clock. They said they would call first thing this morning. For now, let's enjoy the morning," Brody says as he sits back and puts his feet on the firepit.

Abby just stares at him not knowing how much longer she will get to do that.

"Haz, could you call Meg and ask her to come over as soon as she can?" Abby says.

"Sure. Why so early, Abbs?" Hazel says.

Brody hears this one-sided conversation and thinks nothing of it. Is this the new normal? Nobody will believe it if they even try telling someone.

"I just want her here. I want my family together. I don't know how much longer I will be here," Abby says.

"I understand. I will go call her now," Hazel says, getting up to go inside the house.

"Thanks again, Ben, for…oh, and Mom, for letting me stay here for a while. I just didn't want to go through this shit alone," Brody says.

"Hey, bud, I will always be here for you until the day I die. It just so happens your mom is still here, so you have us both. You are never alone, and we all have your back," Ben says.

"Ben, tell him that I am still here for some reason, and now, I firmly believe it is to get him through this. So we got this. This family has been through it, and we will continue to go through this life together," Abby says to Ben.

Ben tells Brody what his mother says.

"Love you, Mom. Love you, Ben. Thank You," Brody says.

"I think I can say this for myself and your mom, we both love you and no need to thank us. That is what we are for," Ben says.

"Okay, okay, who wants more coffee?" Hazel says as she brings out the coffee pot.

She pours Brody another cup.

"One thing I have learned over the years, and I am old so I know, is life is a fucking bitch. You just have to kick that bitch's ass. You know?" Hazel says, looking at Brody.

He laughs as do Abby and Ben, leaving it to Hazel to tell it like it is. She never sugarcoats anything.

"Oh, and Meg is on her way. She said she had planned to come over this morning anyway. Cam is staying with the kids today," Hazel says.

"I don't know what this family would do without you, Haz. You always bring laughter," Abby says.

"No, Abbs. It is the other way around. I wouldn't know what to do without this family. We didn't have much growing up including parental love and guidance, but we always had each other, and that has seemed to get us through. We have been blessed with each other's families," Hazel says as she bends down to give Brody a kiss on the head.

"Love you, kiddo. You are not in this alone," Hazel says.

"I know, and I love all of you too. Could you possibly go in my bathroom and get me another pill? This headache is kicking my ass," Brody asks Hazel.

"You bet. Be right back, and I will make you some food. You need to try and eat, Brods," Hazel says as she goes into the house.

Minutes later, Megan comes outside to see them.

"Hi, guys. Does anyone need anything while I'm up? Hazel is in there making everyone some food. Here's your pill, Brods. Aunt Hazel said you have a horrible headache. Do you need me to do anything?" Megan asks.

"No, I'm good for now. Thanks for bringing me the meds. I can take every four hours. Could you keep track of that? I can't think straight," Brody says.

"Yes, I will set the alarm on my phone," Megan says as she sits down beside him and pulls him in for a hug.

Abby sits and watches them. The two of them have had their problems, and she always wishes they are closer. They love each other, no doubt, and are very protective of one another, but not really that close. She hopes this tragedy will change all that.

"How are you feeling, Ben? Getting enough sleep?" Megan asks.

Megan has always been a caretaker. Abby is so proud of who she has become.

"I am doing okay, Meg. Thank you for always looking out for me," Ben says.

Hazel comes out with sandwiches, salads, chips, and drinks.

"Okay, okay, I am not much of a breakfast maker so lunch it is. We have to stay healthy for each other," Hazel says.

They all laugh, thinking it sure is good to have Hazel there to take the lead.

They all are eating and having a good time when Brody's phone rings. He looks at it and then looks at his family. It is the doctor. He gets up and goes inside to take the call. Hazel reaches out and grabs Abby's hand, and Abby grabs Megan's hand. They are all saying a prayer.

Brody comes back outside with his phone in his hand, and he looks like someone has taken the life right out of him. Abby knows it is bad.

He walks over and says, "Where's Mom?"

Abby gets up and goes to him, grabbing his hand. He feels her warmth and cries. She hugs him, and he just lets her hold him. She touches his face and wipes his tears. He looks up to see his family, and they are all crying. He goes to sit next to Megan, and she hugs him close to her.

"Tell us, Brods, what is it?" Megan says.

He sits up and wipes his tears.

"It's not good, guys. It's cancer, stage four cancer. He called it glioblastoma. They have scheduled me for surgery to remove as much as they can. Surgery is Monday at six thirty in the morning. While I am in surgery, they want to put a port in for the chemo so after I recover from the surgery, I will start radiation and chemo. I ask him what my chances are at beating this thing, and he said he honestly did not know. They would know more after surgery. Worst case is six months," Brody says with tears in his eyes and his lips quivering.

Abby and Megan grab his hands, and they all just cry. He is right this is not good.

"Tell him he has us to get him through. There is not a doubt now that this is why I am still here," Abby says.

Hazel tells Brody what Abby says.

"Mom, you are right because I can't do this without you," Brody says.

Ben kneels before him, putting his hands on his knees and looking in his eyes with tears in his own.

"Brods, I know you are scared, and you have every right to be, but know this, we are all with you and will be with you no matter what is to happen. You and Meg are everything to me, and we will get through this. I love you so damn much, kid," Ben says, crying openly now.

The surgery is Monday, this is Saturday, so they intend to make the most of this weekend for Brody.

"I am going to take some more medicine and lay down for a while, guys," Brody says.

"I will get your meds and get you settled in, Brods," Megan says, and he smiles.

They go into the house, and Abby cries like she has never cried. Hazel and Ben just hold her.

"Why is this happening to him?" Abby wails.

"There is no reason for this shit disease, Abbs. We have each other, and we will get him through this, but you have to stay strong. Get it all out now, all of us, because we cannot do this in front of Brody," Hazel says, and they agree.

"I am going to call John and the kids to let them know what is going on and that I will be staying here indefinitely," Hazel says as she gets up to go in the house.

The Weekend

IT IS A sunny Saturday morning, and they are outside enjoying the day. They all seem to gather outside where the sun is warm. Megan is bringing her family over for a cookout later. The last thing any of them need to do is sit and think about the upcoming challenges for Brody. This gives Abby time to just sit and watch her grandkids that she misses so much. The family decides not to tell Cam or the kids. It is just too much for others to comprehend.

"Who wants breakfast?" Ben asks.

He has always loved to cook.

"Me definitely. I will never turn down anyone cooking for me. Also, Brody needs to eat something with the medicine he is taking," Hazel says.

Brody just looks at her smiles and rolls his eyes. Abby has been by his side all morning, just snuggled in next to him. He feels her next to him and is so comforted by her presence. The kids may not be able to see or hear Abby, but they feel her near them or when she touches them.

"Okay then, breakfast will be ready in a flash," Ben says with a smile on his face.

"Abbs, now I know why when I would call you, you would always be sitting out here. It is not only beautiful. It is so relaxing," Hazel says as she lifts her head to get the sun on her face.

"This used to be my favorite place to be for sure. Ben and I shared many moments in our life and solved all of the world's problems out here," Abby says as she remembers so many moments with Ben.

Brody feels relaxed just listening to Hazel have this one-sided conversation. He may not be able to hear Abby, but he knows exactly what she is saying.

Ben comes out with an amazing breakfast for them—eggs, bacon, sweet rolls, and fruit. Abby watches all of them with peace as they eat and banter with each other.

"Brody, you need to try and eat as much as you can this weekend. Your body will need this reserve for what you are about to go through," Hazel says.

"I know, and I will do my best, Aunt Hazel," Brody says as he picks at his food.

"How is my family this morning?" Megan says as she walks through the back door.

"Meg! Hi, I thought you were coming later for dinner," Hazel says.

"Cam and the kids will be here later, and I just want to spend as much time as I can with all of you during this time. I hope that's okay," Megan says.

"It is more than okay, kiddo. Go grab a plate, and eat some breakfast with us. Glad you are here," Ben says, smiling.

Abby smiles at this. Ben is so good to the kids. She feels so lucky to have had him in her life.

They finish breakfast, and Megan can tell Brody is trying to be strong with his pain.

"Brods, let's go get you some more medicine, and you can lay down for an hour or so? You won't miss a thing. We are just going to clean up and get things ready for the grill out," Megan says.

"Okay, twist my arm. I am feeling tired," Brody says as they get up to go inside.

Abby touches his face as he gets up. He looks back.

"Love you too, Mom," Brody says.

Megan smiles at that.

"I love you too, Mom. I am so glad you are still here," Megan says.

"Abbs, you have some good kids. You did good," Hazel says as the kids go inside.

"It hasn't always been easy. That's for sure. Our lives have been full of challenges, but I wouldn't trade any of the moments we have had together," Abby says to her sister.

Ben is inside cleaning up things in the kitchen. He insists on doing it so Abby and Hazel can have some time.

"This reminds me of Mom and Dad, Haz," Abby says sadly.

Their parents both died of lung cancer, and they have to watch them suffer in the end. It was horrible to go through.

"One thing that is the same, we have each other. It is no doubt going to be a challenge, but, Abby, Brody is strong. Look at what he has been through in his life so far. He is a fighter and will give this his all. We just have to stay strong for him."

Ben comes outside and tells them he needs to go to the store to get things for tonight.

"I'll go with you," Abby says.

"While you two are doing that, I am going to shower," Hazel says.

At the store, Abby gets all the things for a big salad, and Ben picks out the steaks. Ben forgets that he is the only one that can see Abby as he notices people looking at him. To them, he is talking to himself. Abby notices him looking around.

"I'm sorry, Ben. The last thing I want is for people in this town to think you're crazy," Abby says sadly.

"Don't worry about it, Abbs. My time with you is short lived, and I want to be in the moment," Ben says, grabbing her hand.

They continue their time in the store getting everything they need including things that Brody might need while at the hospital.

When Cam and the kids get there, Abby lights up. Boy, how she misses them. She will give anything to hold them and cover their little faces with her kisses. She is blessed to have had them for just a little while. Brody seems to be in good spirits. Hazel and Megan are making sure he is staying up on his pain meds. Abby is so lucky to have all of them to look after him. She can't interact with anyone tonight, not until the kids leave, but she loves just watching her family—the family she created and loves with all of her heart. There is lots of laughter and smiles at dinner. The kids seem to be having a great time. Jackson has brought up his nana more times than not. He misses Abby. The two of them are buddies. Abby gets to spend lots of time with him, Romy, and Maddie. Now, more than ever is she grateful that Megan allows her to be their caregiver when she and Cam work.

It is close to 10:00 p.m. when Megan and Cam leave with the kids. Brody looks beat. He goes to get a shower before bed, and Hazel is getting his medicine ready for him. After his shower, she and Abby are sitting on his bed with him. Bogo is right by his side. Wherever Brody goes, Bogo goes. It seems to help Brody to have his dog through all this.

"Tell Brody that I love him, and I hope he gets a peaceful rest tonight," Abby says.

Hazel tells him, and he smiles.

"I love you too, Mom. I know this is hard for you, but I sure am glad you are still here. Well, sort of here," Brody says, laughing.

Abby leans over and kisses his cheek. He feels that and smiles.

"I don't know about the two of you, but I am tired as hell."

"Good night, sweet boy. Let me know if you need me during the night. I will be here," Hazel says.

Again, that night, Abby sits right there to watch him. She needs him as much as he needs her.

Sunday is here. One more day until surgery, and it is not lost on any of them. When Brody gets up, he and Bogo go out back.

"Good morning all," Brody says as he drinks his coffee.

"Good morning, kiddo," Ben says.

"Hi, darlin'. How did you sleep?" Hazel says.

"Pretty good actually. I just took more pills if you could set your alarm for my next dose," Brody says.

"Will do," Hazel says as she sets her phone alarm.

He sits down next to Hazel, and Abby rubs his head.

"Good morning, Mom," Brody says.

Abby smiles. He may not be able to see her, but he knows she is there.

"Ben, tell him that I will be with him throughout the surgery tomorrow. I will be in there holding his hand and will not leave," Abby says.

Ben tells Brody what his mother says.

"Thanks, Mom. Actually, I was going to ask you to do just that. Knowing you will be with me makes this way less stressful for me, and I mean that," Brody says.

"Brods, we will be waiting for you to be out of recovery. Abby can give us updates throughout. We are all in this with you for the duration of your journey with this stupid, fucking cancer bullshit," Hazel says.

"Aunt Hazel, you always know how to put things in perspective," Brody says, laughing. "Thanks for being here during all of this. I know your family misses you."

"John and the kids understand. If I can be honest, I don't really see the kids that often. They are busy with their own lives, so we try to get together when we can. I have to be here right now. We don't know when Abby will be gone, and I want to make sure you are okay," Hazel says.

Brody feels so lucky to have the family that he has. He sits back with Bogo, enjoying the sunny day.

"What's up bitches?" Megan says as she closes the sliding door to the kitchen.

They all smile at that.

"How is my mini me this morning?" Hazel says to Megan.

Laughing, Megan says, "I am good. Does anyone need anything while I'm up?"

"More coffee please," Brody says, lifting his cup.

Megan grabs his cup and goes inside to fix more coffee.

"I love having everyone here. It brings me so much peace," Abby says.

"We have been blessed, Abbs. There is no doubt about that," Hazel says.

"I second that. What would we do without a patio? We all seem to gravitate to this backyard," Ben says.

"It's peaceful out here. It gets wonderful sunlight and with all of my flowers it makes for beautiful scenery," Abby says.

Megan comes back out with the coffee refilling all their cups.

"How nervous are you, Brods? Do you need me to do anything for you today to get ready for tomorrow? Laundry? Pack a bag for the hospital? Anything?" Megan says.

"Actually, yes, all of that, please," he says, smiling at Megan.

Megan has always spoiled him. She is always a little mother when it comes to her brother.

"Okay, I will get your laundry done and pack a bag for you. No problem," Megan says.

They spend the rest of the day talking, laughing, and telling stories of the past. Megan is in Brody's room finishing up with his bag.

"There you go. You are all ready for tomorrow. I will meet you guys at the hospital in the morning," Megan says, sitting on the bed next to Brody.

She turns to look at him.

"Brods, I love you so much. Never forget that. You are so strong. You will get through this, and I will be right by your side. Look at what we have been through in our lives, and here we are. I mean who else can say their mom is a ghost?" Megan says with a nervous laugh.

"True on that one. Thank you for all you have done and do on a daily basis for me, Megs. I love you, Cam, and the kids so damn much. Look, I don't know how this will end, but please don't forget how much I love you. I never told you this, but I have always looked up to you my whole life. Sometimes a little jealous because you always have seemed to have your life together when I was such a screwup. The best part is you never treated me like a screwup. You always made me believe anything is possible and I could do and be anything. You made me want to be a better person. You are, hands down, the best sister on the planet," Brody says as tears stream down his face.

"Well, thanks for making me cry, Brods. I happen to think that God gave me the best brother in the world. Thank you. I love you so much," Megan says as she hugs him tight.

"Okay, okay, I will see you in the morning. Try to get some sleep tonight," Megan says, leaving the room.

She gives everyone hugs and goes home for the day.

Abby, Hazel, and Ben go in to tell Brody good night and to give him hugs.

"I am turning in too. Good night, guys. See you in the morning," Hazel says to Abby and Ben.

"Good night, Haz. Sleep well," Abby says.

"Let's go snuggle," Abby says, pulling Ben to the couch.

The two of them sit for hours, talking and crying. Ben doesn't care what time it is. He can sleep when Abby is gone. For now, he needs to be with her each and every second. He falls asleep intertwined in her legs. The love they have for each other is unfailing. Abby just watches him as he sleeps, knowing and feeling she will not be here much longer.

Surgery Day

THE MORNING COMES, and it is time for Brody to go back to surgery. They all get to hug and kiss him. He is feeling loopy from the sedatives they give him. Standing in the hallway, they all watch him leave. Abby is with him and will stay with him during the surgery. As they are getting him prepped and ready, Abby kisses him on the forehead and hugs him. Brody feels her do this and smiles.

"Thanks, Mom, for being here with me. I love you so much," Brody says.

She squeezes his hand as tears stream down her face.

"It has been over an hour. We should have been updated by now," Megan says.

"Hang in there, Megs. Abby will update us soon," Hazel says.

Ben just sits there quiet. He has been praying all morning.

"Brody deserves good things in his life. He has come too far for any of this crap," Ben says as he gets up to go for a walk.

Megan and Hazel just look at him. They are all worried.

Abby comes out, and Hazel stands up to give her a hug.

"Any news?" Hazel asks.

Megan stands up even though she can't see her mom. She wants to be close. Abby grabs Megan's hand.

"It is taking longer than they expected. The tumor is wrapped around some layers in the brain. They are having to go about it very carefully and slow. He is handling it like a champ," Abby says.

"We are praying for him, Abbs," Hazel says.

"Where is Ben?" Abby asks.

"He went for a walk," Hazel says.

Abby squeezes Megan's hand.

"I better get back in there. I will let you know if anything new arises. Love you guys," Abby says as she leaves the two of them.

"Love you, Abbs. Hang in there," Hazel says.

Ben gets back, and Hazel tells him what Abby says. Hazel looks over at Meg, and she is sleeping. She has been through so much lately with Abby's passing and coming back, her job, kids, and now Brody. Hazel knows she will be okay, but she won't leave until she is sure of it.

Two more hours go by and still nothing. Megan brings work, and she is keeping herself busy with that. Hazel brings a book, and she just about has it finished. Ben plays a card game on his phone. Each one is trying not to think about what can be going on. Megan thinks about her mom. She doesn't think she will recover from her death now finding out she is somewhat still here. Megan feels her mother's presence when she is nearby. She feels her touch. That gives Megan so much comfort. What will it be like when she is no longer here at all? Megan feels much stronger than she has in the past. She knows things will be okay. Definitely not what they used to be, but things will be okay. She prays that Brody will be okay. Surely, God won't take two people she loves. That will be more than she can bear. As she thinks of all of the times she and Brody have with their mom, tears stream down her face. She needs her brother to be okay. He has to be.

Abby comes out, and Ben and Hazel both stand up. Megan sees them stand and so does she.

"They are just closing up. He did great, and they got it all," Abby says.

Hazel tells Megan what Abby says. They all cry with relief. It has been agony waiting on this news.

"Now, the hard part begins with recovery and treatments. Brace yourselves for what is to come. I am going to stay with Brody. I will see you all in his room."

Abby hugs Ben tightly. "I love you so much," Abby says through her tears.

"I love you too, Abbs," Ben says.

She looks at Hazel and Megan, grabbing them both for a hug.

"Love you both so much," Abby says.
Hazel tells Megan what is said.
"I love you too, Mom," Megan says.
"Love you, Abbs. Stay strong in there," Hazel says to her sister.

Recovery

BRODY SPENDS OVER a week in the hospital and now is home with the family. They have a routine. Hazel and Megan help him with his physical therapy, and Ben does all the cooking. Abby wants so badly to be a part of all this. She sits with Brody at night, making sure he is okay. Brody knows she is there. He can always feel her presence.

"Let's go, kiddo. You can do this," Hazel says to Brody as he does his balance exercises.

"I am so sick of this shit," Brody says.

"I know you are, but stay strong. You got this," Hazel says.

They finish up the exercises, and Ben has lunch ready for them.

"It's that time again, Brods," Ben says, handing him his medicine.

"Thanks, Ben," Brody says as he takes the meds.

They all seem to gather outside. It is their sanctuary, their calm. Abby sits next to Brody, rubbing his hair. Brody smiles.

"Mom, you never stop being a mom, even when you are technically dead," Brody says, laughing.

"We are the only family on the planet that could find any humor in that," Hazel says.

"Okay, chemo and radiation start on Friday. This is Wednesday. The plan is Ben and I will take him to those sessions, and I will sit in with him. Hazel, you and Megs can get the house in order and the grocery shopping done while we do that. We can all take turns with Brody needing things throughout the day and night after chemo. I think we are doing a good job with keeping him up on his meds. If he is not in any pain, then his therapy goes much better," Abby says.

"Sounds like a good plan, Abbs. Try not to worry. We are all here for each other," Hazel says.

"What plan has Mom come up with?" Brody says, looking at Hazel.

She tells him what Abby says, and he laughs.

"Mom, you always have to plan out everything, don't you? I guess that's why our lives always ran smooth growing up," Brody says.

Abby nods her head in agreement, thinking that they would have never made it through without her when, in fact, she sees they all are making it just fine. This gives her mixed emotions. She loves that they all know how to do life with or without her, but she wants them to need her. A mother always wants to feel needed no matter how old her kids get.

Megan walks out back. "How is my family today?" she says.

"All is good here, Megs. Hey, how are the kids and Cam? I feel like I haven't spent any time with them," Brody says.

"Well, you haven't, but you get a free pass. I mean you are only trying to stay alive right now. On another note, I have come up with a plan to get through the chemo and radiation," Megan says.

"Let me stop you right there, Megs. Mom already has a plan in place. I swear the two of you are so much alike," Brody says.

Abby reaches out and grabs Megan's hand. Megan looks down at her hand.

"Great minds think alike, Mom. I love you," Megan says.

Abby gives her hand a squeeze.

"Well, okay, then I guess Mom's plan it is," Megan says.

"Have you eaten lunch yet, kiddo? There is plenty left," Ben says.

"Actually, I grabbed some on the way over. Thanks though," Megan says.

"Well, I am going to go lay down for a while. This medicine is kicking my ass. Megs, are you up for reading more of that book you got me?" Brody asks.

"Well, of course. That's why I brought it. You know you are spoiled, right?" Megan says.

"Hey, being the baby has its advantages. I have to milk it," Brody says, laughing.

"You two go do that, and I will get the laundry and house finished," Hazel says.

"And I will get the lawn mowed before the neighbors have a riot," Ben says.

That leaves Abby sitting there.

Megan is at the door and turns around. She has no idea where her mom is, but she says, looking around, "Mom, would you want to come with Brody and me? Listen in on the book?"

Abby gets up and goes to her, hugging her tight.

"I will take that as a yes. Let's go," Megan says.

Abby lies with Brody, listening to Megan reading the book. Megan is such a wonderful person. She will do anything for her family. Abby's heart swells with pride. As Abby is listening to the book, her mind drifts to thoughts of her parents. She knows she will see them in Heaven as they are firm believers of God, but will they be the same? Will they be better? Growing up, they don't have much time for their kids. Her mom always says, "Your father comes first," and that he does. Abby and her sisters are an afterthought most of the time. Thank goodness she always has Hazel. Hazel has been her savior for all of her life. Abby shakes her head back to reality. Why would she all of the sudden think of her parents? She has been thinking of many things lately and most of it has to do with her past.

Megan looks up from the book she is reading and sees that Brody is asleep.

"Mom," she whispers.

Abby squeezes her arm, and Megan smiles. They both get up to let Brody sleep. Ben is still mowing, and Hazel is finishing up in the kitchen.

"Mom, will you stay in here with me while I get some things together for dinner?" Megan asks.

"Of course, I will. I am right here, sweet girl," Abby says.

Hazel tells Megan what she says. For the life of them, they can't figure out why Ben and Hazel are the only ones who can see or hear Abby. Maybe they will never know why. Abby sits and watches

Megan get things ready for the recipe she is trying tonight. Megan is so much like Abby. She has Abby's soft and caring heart. She loves to cook like Abby, and most importantly, she is a wonderful mother to Abby's sweet grandbabies. Oh, let's not forget Megan's wicked sense of humor. She will cut you to shreds and make it funny.

"Aunt Hazel, how are John and the kids doing without you being home?" Megan asks.

"Well, John is keeping busy with work and his garden. The kids have their own lives. I really didn't see them much. Life gets busy, and they have their own families," Hazel says with a hint of sadness.

"I am busy too, but Mom and I always found time to spend together. It was important to me to have that relationship with her," Megan says this and starts to cry.

"I'm sorry I find myself crying in the strangest moments. I know you are kind of here, Mom, but not really. Not to Brody and me. I can feel your presence, but just not see you. I guess what I am saying is I really fucking miss you," Megan says through her tears.

Hazel tears up listening to her niece. She feels for her and wishes she could take that pain away.

"I love you so much, Megs. Trust me, this is not what I thought my life would end up like. I know this is hard. I do. I also now know that Brody is the reason I have stuck around," Abby says, and Hazel repeats this to Megan.

"I think so too, Mom. I just wish things were different. That's all," Megan says.

"We all do, babe. We all do. One thing I know about this family is we can get through anything," Hazel says.

"I just miss my best friend. You know? Some days are better than others, of course. I have been lucky to have had such a close relationship with you, Mom. I hope that I will have the same with my kids," Megan says.

"You most certainly will. Your kids are the luckiest kids on the planet to have you for a mom," Abby says, crying.

"Sure, Abbs, make me repeat that when you are crying. Ugh. She's crying, Megs," Hazel says as she tells Megan what is said.

"Can you hug me, Mom? I just need to feel your arms around me," Megan says.

Abby walks over and hugs her daughter with all of her might. The love that she has for her children is like no other love.

They all hear it. It was a loud yell, a screeching yell. They know its Brody, and they all go running in to see what has happened. He is sitting up in bed, holding his head.

"Make it go away, Mom. I hurt so bad," Brody says.

"Go get his medicine and some water, Haz," Abby says.

She sits down and holds him and rubbing his head. He calms down and looks up to see Megan.

"I am going to get the heat pad. Remember the doctor said that could ease some of the pain?" Megan says as she leaves to go get it.

Hazel comes back and gives him two pills with his water.

"Thanks, Aunt Hazel," Brody says as he takes the medicine.

Megan comes back in, plugs in the heat pad, and tells Brody to lay his head on it. He is calm.

"I will sit with him and rub his head. You and Meg can finish what you were doing," Abby says to Hazel.

They leave to go and finish up in the kitchen. Abby sits by him on the bed, rubbing his head and temples. Her sweet boy. It breaks her heart to see him in all that pain. The medicine and heat seem to be helping. He is much calmer.

"Thanks, Mom, for being here and being with me. I don't want you to worry about me getting addicted to all of the pills I am taking. I know you have thought it. I promise you I will not let my life go down a path of addiction again," Brody says as he drifts off to sleep.

He has fought so hard to be the person he is today. He is strong, smart, loving, kind, and, most of all, clean from all of the drugs that once ruled his mind. Abby is proud of who he has become. She loves this kid so damn much.

Abby goes back into the kitchen, and Ben is there with the girls. It looks like he just showered. Abby walks up to him, giving him a kiss.

"You smell good," Abby says.

"Why, thank you, ma'am. How's Brods?" Ben says.

"He is asleep. Oh, we need to up his medicine to three every four hours," Abby says.

"Will do, and I have the timer set on my phone," Hazel says.

"I love all of you very much. Dinner is ready whenever you get hungry. I have to get home and get the kids fed and bathed. I will be here tomorrow," Megan says as she hugs each of them.

"Want to go on a walk with me?" Ben asks Abby.

Abby looks at Hazel not really knowing if she should leave Brody.

"You guys go do that. I will go sit with Brody. I need to call John anyway," Hazel says.

They get the dogs and are on their way.

"I know you are worried about Brody, Abbs. He has all of us for support. Things will get better," Ben says.

"I am worried. Also, I don't know how much longer I will be here. I just need everyone to be okay before I am gone," Abby says.

"Abbs, we are okay. When you died suddenly, it was horrible. I am not sure I would have ever recovered from that. Seeing you now and having time to get that closure is the best thing that has ever happened to us. Will we miss you when you are gone? Every single minute. You are everything to this family. You are our rock. You make everything right in the world. The love that you have given to each and every one of us will get us through until we see you again," Ben says, squeezing her hand in his.

"I love you, Ben. I have loved you since the day we met. I know that as long as you are alive, you will make sure the kids are good. You have always taken such good care of us. For that, I am forever grateful. So I will tell you what I'll do. I will pick out the best mansion for us in Heaven and will wait for you until the end of time," Abby says, laughing.

"Well, it had better be a good one, Mrs. Stevens. Only the best for me," Ben says as he scoops her in his arms.

Chemo Starts

SUN GLARING INTO the window, Brody opens his eyes, groaning from the awful throb in his head. He thinks something went wrong with the surgery, and nobody is telling him that. Why would he feel so much pain if it went as planned? It just doesn't make sense to him. He knows he has to get up and shower. Today is his first chemo session. He can hear his family outside. As families go, he definitely has the best. He and Megan haven't always been close, and that is his fault. Drugs have a way of sucking the life right out of you. He doesn't remember half of his life, and that is because he chose drugs over life. Thank goodness his family doesn't give up on him or he would be dead, and that is a fact.

"Those are nice thoughts to wake up to, Brods," he says out loud to himself, getting up and getting in the shower.

"You're awfully quiet this morning, Abbs. What's up?" Hazel says.

"Just thinking and praying. I just want things to go well for Brody. I just can't wrap my head around that he is now clean and sober. Now, he has to go through this. I guess there are things in this life that we will never understand. I can remember Mom always saying "life isn't fair," and she was most definitely right about that," Abby says.

"I know things are shitty right now, Abbs, but don't listen to the shit Mom used to say. Did she ever have any positivity? Come on, things will get better. Stay positive. Brody needs all positive vibes right now," Hazel says.

"Good morning all," Brody says, walking into the kitchen.

"Good morning, sweetheart," Hazel says.

"Good morning, kiddo," Ben says.

"I'm here, I'm here," Megan says, walking into the kitchen. "I wanted to be here before you left, Brods," Megan says, hugging her brother.

"Thanks, Megs. That means a lot," Brody says.

"Here are some cards that the kids made you. I told them they could visit you in a day or two," Megan says, handing Brody the cards.

He looks through the cards with a big smile on his face.

"Oh, I just took my medicine, if you could set a timer for the next dose please," Brody says to Megan.

"Will do, but you may want to take them with you today. Radiation doesn't take long, but the chemo is four hours according to your sheet," Megan says.

"I will hang on to them for you, Brody, and Megan can let me know when it's time for your next dose," Ben says.

"Okay, I will go grab them," Brody says.

"Megan and I will be here getting things done. If you guys need anything, let us know," Hazel says to Abby.

"We will. Thank you both of you for all you do," Abby says.

Hazel tells Megan what her mom says.

"Mom, hang in there. I love you so much," Megan says out loud not knowing where to look.

Abby reaches out and gives Megan's hand a squeeze.

"All right, folks, let's get this show on the road," Brody says, handing Ben his meds.

"Okay, kiddo, let's go kick this cancers ass," Ben says.

Ben, Abby, and Brody all leave to get to his appointment. First stop is radiation. This first visit takes a little longer than normal. They have to get things set up for where the radiation needs to hit. The next visits will be in and out. They promise him.

The three of them head down the hall for his chemo session. He fills out all of the necessary paperwork, and they call his name to take him back. He looks over at Ben.

"Will you come with me?" Brody asks.

"You bet," Ben says as he looks at Abby, and she smiles.

They all go back with him. Abby and Ben sit listening to what they are going to do, how long it takes, and how often he will have to do this. They tell him he will be on a dose-dense schedule, meaning less time in between sessions. For the time being, he will have his chemo sessions once a week. They have called in medicine to help with nausea and vomiting. They get the IV inserted and give him a dose of aprepitant. This will help with the nausea they tell him. After that, they start with the chemotherapy. They tell him this will take three hours.

"Well, here we go. It's gonna be a helluva ride," Brody says.

Abby sits nervously just watching him.

"I brought some cards if you want to play," Ben says.

"Yes, please, anything to make time go quicker," Brody says.

Abby grabs his hand and gives it a squeeze.

"It will be okay, Mom. I love you," Brody tells her.

Abby rubs his head.

Abby watches the two of them play cards. They always have good laughs with each other. Ben has been such a good father to both of her kids. She feels blessed to have had him on her side. She can't help but stare at the poison that is being pumped into her baby boy. It makes her heart break, knowing he has to go through any of this. She wishes she could be here, really here with him. She forces herself not to think about the whys. Why did this all happen? Why is she not here for her family? She blocks all that out because a force much bigger than her makes these decisions. Brody suddenly puts his cards down and closes his eyes.

"Are you okay, buddy?" Ben says.

"My head," Brody says.

Ben reaches into his coat pocket to get the medicine. Abby tells him to give him three of them. Ben goes to get him some water and gives the pills to him.

"I just need to close my eyes for a bit, Ben. Can we finish cards later?" Brody asks.

"Of course, you just rest, Brods. Your mother and I are right here if you need us," Ben says.

"Mom, could you rub my head, please?" Brody asks.

Abby reaches over and starts rubbing his head, and she can feel Brody relax as soon as she does this.

Ben watches Abby with Brody, and her love has always been unfailing with her kids. When Brody was going through his addiction, it was hard for Ben to accept that it was a disease, and he wanted Brody to snap out of it, grow up. He and Abby have numerous fights about it. Ben just does not understand any of it at the time. Ben knows now that Brody is doing the best he can. He also knows that Brody still struggles with it to this day. He is proud of him for getting through it and wishes he could turn back the clock. He would have been a better dad to him during that time. He would have been a better husband for Abby. He knows her heart is broken, and he just keeps on with his bullshit. He doesn't help her when she needs it. He adds to her pain. This is something he will never forgive himself for. When Abby loves you, she is all in, and there is no in between. She will fight for you until the end. He knows this now.

The three of them get home, and Brody is beat. He looks defeated. It has been a long day for him, and his head is pounding.

"Hey, guys, how did it go? By the looks of you, Brods, not well," Hazel said.

"Yeah, I'm sure I look as good as I feel," Brody says, taking his coat off.

"How about I get the heat pad ready, and you go lay down for a while. I can read your book to you," Megan says.

"I would love that, Megs. Mom, I hate to sound like a baby, but you come with us and rub my head? It really helps," Brody says.

Abby squeezes his hand, and he smiles.

"You guys go do that, and I will make a little dinner for everyone. I will make you some soup, Brods. You need something in your system," Hazel says.

They go get Brody settled in while Hazel and Ben go to the kitchen.

"So you want to tell me how it really went? Even you look beat up, Ben," Hazel says.

"It just sucks seeing him go through this. Watching Abby with Brody today just brought back some old shit. I was a real asshole to

Brody and Abby when he was going through his life just trying to survive. I can't shake my guilt. I know they don't hold it against me. I hold it against myself," Ben says.

"So far, all I hear is you, you, you. It wasn't about you then, and it's not now. Look, I remember it well when Brody was going through his addiction struggles, you were not there for him or Abby. You were pissed off at the world. You were and are a good dad to those kids. Nothing you did caused his addiction. Those are his demons. Stop taking ownership for it. He needed you then, and you chose to be an asshole. He needs you now, and you choose to be there for him. All we have is now. Unfortunately, we can't turn back time. I, for one, would have turned it back long ago. We have all done things we are not proud of. Just try to be the best you can today. All we have is today Ben," Hazel says.

"You are right. You always did tell me like it is. You never hold back. I love you for it, Haz. Thanks you," Ben says.

"Okay, how about you pour us a drink?" Hazel says, laughing.

"Brody is sleeping. Mom is still in there with him. I have to get going you guys. I have kids to feed and give baths. Please call me if you need anything at all. I will be here in the morning to help out and spend time with Mom. Love you guys so much," Megan says as she hugs each of them.

"Love you too, kiddo. Thank you for all you do," Ben says.

"Love you, sweetheart. We got a lot done today, and I couldn't have done it without you," Hazel says.

Abby comes in a little later and tells them Brody is still sleeping.

"We are going to have to wake him in thirty minutes. He needs his meds for pain and nausea. We have to keep up on it, or we will have real problems on our hands," Hazel says.

"Let's eat, and we will get him squared away," Ben says, pouring him and Hazel another round.

Abby sits with them as they eat.

"I hate seeing him like this. Nobody wants to see their children hurting or in pain. With him, it seems different. He is again fighting for his life. I mean, it all seems a little unfair, doesn't it?" Abby says sadly.

"Yes, it is totally unfair. He is a good kid and deserves all the happiness this world can give him, but we don't make the rules of this crazy life. I am a firm believer that life is a total bitch. It will always be a bitch. I also think it's our job to kick this bitch right in the ass!" Hazel says.

"Leave it to you to come up with life lessons of the world," Abby says.

"You are welcome," Hazel says, lifting her glass.

Ben says he will clean up the dishes while Abby and Hazel go to get Brody up to take his meds and have some soup. Brody is sitting up in his bed with tears in his eyes. Bogo sits right by his side, looking at him with concern.

"What's wrong, babe?" Hazel says.

"I hurt, and the only way it stops for just a little while is with all the pills. I'm scared. What if I make through it all of this, and I am right back to where I was with all the drugs?" Brody says.

Abby sits by his side on the bed and grabs his hand. He smiles through the tears.

"Look, Brods, you need to focus on one thing at a time. You need these pills to survive. If you don't take them, you won't make it. Stop feeling guilty about getting yourself through this hurtle. After we get you through this shit, we will tackle the addiction. That's only if it is a problem. Now, you need to take these pills and remember it is for your survival. You are doing nothing wrong," Hazel says.

"Thanks, Aunt Hazel," Brody says, taking the pills.

"Can you try to eat some of this soup?" Hazel asks.

Brody takes the soup and starts to eat. He eats most of the soup.

"I'm going to sit outside for a while. I need some fresh air," Brody says.

"Great idea. We will join you. The sun is going down. I will get your jacket. Remember the doctor said to avoid the sun while you are going through chemo. You need to be careful," Abby says.

Hazel tells him what she says.

"Will do, Mom," Brody says.

Sitting outside, they are all silent, soaking up the last of the sun for the day. Sometimes, just sitting together in silence is enough.

Brody watches Ben playing with all the dogs. He wishes he had enough energy to play with Bogo or take him for a walk. Bogo has been a lifesaver. They save each other, no doubt about it.

Sitting there listening to his family talk is comforting. Brody is enjoying his time outside until he wasn't. He gets up and runs full speed into the house. Abby, Hazel, and Ben follow him in the house. They find him in his bathroom. He is vomiting so violently. It scares all of them. Abby starts rubbing his back.

"Let's get a wet cloth for him, Haz," Abby says.

"I'm on it," she says.

They know something like this can happen with the chemo. They are hoping it won't be so bad. After he gets done, he doesn't have the energy to move from the bathroom floor. Ben carries him to his bed. Hazel is wiping his head down.

"I hurt so bad, Mom. My head feels like it may explode," Brody says, shutting his eyes.

"We have the patches to give you if you can't keep the meds down, and obviously, you're not keeping anything down. I will go get them," Hazel says.

Abby gets the heat pad and lays his head on it. She rubs the top of his head and temples. He seems to be calming a little. Hazel gets back with the patches.

"This one is for nausea, and it is a strong one," she says as she places it on his shoulder. "This one is for the pain, buddy. It is also a strong one," she says, placing it on his other shoulder. "These are good for six hours. I will set a timer to keep track of when to replace them," Hazel says.

Ben comes in with a glass of ice water and sits it on his nightstand. Bogo is by his side, looking very worried about his best friend.

"We will be in the kitchen, Abbs, if he needs anything else," Hazel says as she and Ben leave him to rest.

Abby sits by his side, rubbing his head. Tears stream down her face, and for once, she is grateful her sweet boy can't see her. A mother's job is to protect her children against any harm. Abby sits with frustration, knowing all this is out of her control, just like his addiction is out of her control. As much as she wants to help him, she can't, and now she finds herself in the same position. Abby closes her eyes and prays—prays long and hard for God to spare her son's life against this horrible disease. She has to believe that he doesn't get through the challenge of his addictions only to die from this bullshit cancer.

They spend the next three hours with him as he is getting sick. Will it ever stop? Every time he would throw up, his head would be in agonizing pain. Finally, as Abby is rubbing his head, he drifts into a sleep. She just sits there staring at his breathing. He opens his eyes.

"You're make everything better, Mom. You always have," Brody says as he goes back to sleep.

Abby can't keep the tears from falling. She wishes she could take away all this sickness and pain. Mothers should be able to do that. That should be their superpower.

Hazel walks in and sees Abby crying and bends down near her sister to hold her. She knows how much her kids mean to her. This whole thing is unfair. She should be here in person for Brody. This has to be a cruel joke. Abby lets her sister comfort her. She needs her.

"I am going to stay up until he needs his patches changed, and then I will turn in. If you need me, I will be up. Ben is watching TV in the living room if you need him," Hazel says.

"Thanks, Haz. I will be in there with you guys in just a minute," Abby says.

Walking in the living room, Abby sees Ben watching a movie. He looks up and smiles. Just seeing her melts his heart. He scoots over, and she lies by him, putting her head on his shoulder.

"It's not fair, Ben. Seeing him like that is torture," Abby says.

"I know, I know. Stay strong, Abbs. This is where the rubber meets the road. This is where he will need you to get him through. You said that you know in your heart the reason you have not crossed over is this. To help him get through this. Get your game face on babe. You got this. As hard as it is going to be, you got this," Ben says, kissing her forehead.

Hazel gets his patches changed and sets her alarm for the next dose. Abby doesn't know what they will do without her. She has been a lifesaver for her family. Abby stays with Brody through the night, making sure he is okay. He does better than she thinks. She loves watching Bogo with Brody. The love that dog has for him is incredible. Bogo just lay by his side all night, giving Brody healthy vibes through the night.

Hazel comes in six hours later with more patches. Brody opens his eyes this time.

"Thanks, Aunt Hazel," he says with a faint smile.

She looks at him and gives her biggest smile.

"You bet, sweet boy. How has your night been?" Hazel asks.

"Good I think. I am pretty sure Mom has been here all night," Brody says.

Abby gives him a squeeze.

"You would be right, kiddo. She has been with you nonstop. Do you feel up to some oatmeal or an egg? Something easy?" she asks.

"Ugh. *No* please, and I can't even think about it right now," he says.

"Okay, I understand, but we have to watch and not go down the rabbit hole of not eating. That's when real problems start. Ben stocked up on the shakes that the hospital said to get. You need to at least try to drink those. Okay?" Hazel says.

"Yes, ma'am. Will do. I am going to slowly get myself a shower, and I will meet you guys in the kitchen for that yummy shake," Brody says.

"Wise guy," Hazel says, rolling her eyes.

They are all gathered in the kitchen bright and early. Hazel is on her second cup of coffee. Ben is making some breakfast. Brody comes in moving slow.

"Well, I did shower, but I think I have to go back to bed," he says as he sits in the chair.

"Let me go change the bedding and get things all freshened up before you do," Hazel says as she heads that way.

Ben hands him a shake.

"I know it's not appealing to you, but try to drink as much as you can. It has all the nutrients in it that you need," Ben says.

"Thanks, Ben. I will do my best," Brody says.

"How are the patches working? Better than the pills?" Ben asks.

"They are a helluva a lot stronger that's for sure. So yes, to answer your question. Much better," Brody says.

"All right, B, you are all ready to go in there. I even put a diffuser in there with some lavender. That is supposed to relax you," Hazel says, rubbing his head.

"Just in time. I feel like I am going to pass out," Brody says.

Ben runs over to him just in case and helps him back to bed. He has never felt so weak in his life. They all go in Brody's room to get him settled in.

"I noticed you didn't drink any of that shake. You have to try to at least do that, kiddo," Ben says.

"I know. I just can't right now. The thought of anything makes me want to vomit. I have been taking sips of water," Brody says.

"Hi, guys. Are we all just going to hang in Brody's room today?" Megan says, laughing.

"We were just getting him back to bed. He says he is too weak to be anywhere else," Hazel says, giving Megan a hug.

Abby reaches over to give Megan a squeeze. Megan smiles.

"Hi, Mom," she says.

"Megs, you feel up to reading more of the book?" Brody asks.

"You want to do that or I could put a movie on for us?" Megan asks.

"Honestly, my head feels so dizzy that I don't think I could focus on a movie," he says.

"Book it is. Let me go get a glass of water, and I will be right back," Megan says.

"I am going to shower while we have everything under control here," Hazel says to the group.

"I need to run to the store and pick up a few things. I will be back shortly. Love you," Ben says to Abby, giving her a kiss on his way out.

Abby just sits on the edge of Brody's bed. It looks like her family has everything under control. She knows right then and there that they will be just fine without her. They are a strong bunch. It is like Brody is reading her mind. He reaches out his hand.

"Mom?" he says.

She scoots closer to him and rubs his head.

"We will always need you. No matter what we go through in our lives or how many years have passed since your death. There will not be a day this family won't need you," he says with a faint smile.

Abby leans over him and hugs him tight. He loves to feel her near. It is a calm that he has never felt before.

"I love you too, Momma," he says.

He always calls her that when he wants to melt her heart. It works every time.

Megan comes back and settles in beside her brother.

"Okay, everyone ready for where we left off? I know Mom is in here. I feel her presence," Megan says.

"Yep, you would be correct. Thanks for rubbing my head, Mom. It does make a difference," he says.

"Oh please, even dead Mom still spoils you. Sorry, Mom, but it's true. We have all spoiled this kid," Megan says, laughing.

She starts to read, and Abby just looks at her children. They have both grown into remarkable human beings.

Second Chemo Day

"GOOD MORNING, BEAUTIFUL," Ben says as he walks into the kitchen.

Abby looks up at him and smiles.

"That never gets old. Good morning to you," she says.

"Ugh, please you two," Hazel says, rolling her eyes.

It's been two weeks since his last chemo session.

"Don't forget Brody had his scan this morning before his chemo session," Abby says to Ben.

He nods his head.

"Good morning all," Brody says, walking into the kitchen.

"Good morning, kiddo," Ben and Hazel say in unison.

Nobody says it, but they all notice that he has lost weight—weight that he doesn't have to lose in the first place.

"Ready for your shake?" Hazel says to him.

"Do I have to?" he says.

"Unfortunately, yes. I know you have zero appetite, but try and at least drink your shakes. It will help you so much," Hazel says, handing him the shake.

He takes it and tries to drink as much as he can without vomiting. He hasn't really had a "good" day since his first chemo session, and now he has to have another one.

"Good morning, bubs," Megan says as she walks into the kitchen.

She walks over and gives her brother a big hug.

"Hey, Megs," Brody says.

She notices that he seems weak. She looks concerned at her Aunt Hazel.

"I will get the house all cleaned and Brody's room sanitized so everything will be ready when you guys get back," Hazel says.

"I will make dinner for everyone, and it will be ready when you get back. You can warm it up when you're ready to eat," Megan says.

"Thanks, everyone. I love that this family always takes care of each other," Abby says.

"Abbs, that's what family is for. I, for one, am here until I am not needed anymore," Hazel says.

"Oh, Aunt Hazel, we always need you," Brody says, laughing.

"Well, then I guess I should just move in with you, Brods," Hazel says, smiling.

"Um, on second thought…," Brody laughs.

Hazel gives him a little push. Abby notices that no matter what he goes through, he never loses his sense of humor.

"Well, let's get this over with. Mom, you're coming with me, right?" Brody asks.

Abby gives his hand a squeeze, and he smiles.

"Good. Let's go," he says.

Brody goes in for the scan. It doesn't take too long. He then goes upstairs to do his chemo session. This will be three hours long. He wishes that he could see and talk to Abby through this, but her being there and feeling her presence have been comforting. Ben and Abby both go in with him during the chemo. Abby watches as he and Ben play cards. He has just started to lose his hair. It makes Abby so sad to see her baby like this. He has to get through this. He just has to.

An hour left to go on the session, and Brody stops playing cards. He says he needs to close his eyes to see if it will help his head. Headaches and dizziness have become his new normal. He lies back with his eyes shut, and Abby starts to rub his head.

"Thanks, Mom," Brody says.

Abby kisses his forehead.

In the car on the way home, Brody says, "Two more sessions to go. Piece of cake. I'm totally kicking cancer's ass."

He doesn't say this very convincing.

"You are definitely a strong person, Brody. I am in awe of how you have handled all of this," Ben says.

They see Bogo run to the car as they pull in the driveway.

"Someone is glad to see me," Brody says.

They all go into the kitchen to see Hazel and Megan. Megan is finishing up dinner.

"Hey, Brods, how'd it go?" Megan asks.

"It went. I feel like I ran a marathon. I am so tired. Before I head in for a nap, could you do something for me, Megs?" Brody asks.

"Anything," she says.

"Shave my head. Please," he says.

With tears in her eyes, Megan agrees to do it. They go in his bathroom, and Megan gets the clippers out.

"Are you sure you want to do this?" she asks.

"Yes, I am sick of seeing my hair on the pillow. It is way too depressing. So let's do this thing," he says.

With her hand shaking, she starts shaving her brother's head.

"Hey, not bad, Little Brother. You look handsome," Megan says.

"Well, of course I do. I mean, did you think my hair made me?" he says, laughing.

"When do you think Mom will leave?" Brody asks.

"I don't think it's up to her. I'm sure she doesn't even know," Megan says.

"It has been good having her sort of here. The pain of her death doesn't seem so bad. You know?" he says.

"Yeah, I do know. It's like she is transitioning us from not having her here at all. It is all so bizarre. To feel her when she touches us. It is like all the love in the world. That is what it feels like when she hugs me," Megan says.

"I think that's why my head feels so much better when she rubs it. It is a calm I have never felt. I could not be going through this without her. That is a fact," he says.

Abby, Ben, and Hazel all walk into Brody's room to see what he now looks like. Abby goes over to him, hugging him, and then rubs his bald head.

"I know, Mom. Pretty handsome, huh?" he says.

"You look amazing, kid," Hazel says.

"I second that," Ben says.

"Thanks for doing this, Megs," Brody says.

"You are welcome. Love you, bub," she says.

"I am going to lay down. I feel exhausted," Brody says.

"Let's get those patches changed before you lay down. Also, your doctor called in some pills for you to take. Ben is going to pick them up, and I will wake you up to take them," Hazel says.

"My duties are done here. I am going to head out and relieve Cam and get dinner done. Love you guys, and I will see you tomorrow. Call me if you need me for anything," Megan says, leaving.

Ben leaves to pick up Brody's medicine. Abby and Hazel decide to sit outside.

"I hate not being seen or heard by the kids. I miss my grandbabies so much. I think the whole thing of me still being here is torture," Abby says sadly.

"Oh, it for sure sucks. I mean, what in the hell have you done wrong in your life to deserve this bullshit? Nothing that's what. You are the best person I know. God must have a plan for this. Trust it, and go with it. It's all you have right now. I'm glad I can see you and still talk to you," Hazel says.

"How long are you going to stay, Haz? I'm sure John misses you like crazy."

"He does no doubt, but he also knows I need to be here right now. I don't know how long I'll be here. Depends on you. I want to be here while you are still here. When do you think they will call about Brody's scan?" Hazel asks.

"I would say tomorrow for sure. If not today," Abby says.

"I forgot to tell you that a neighbor lady stopped by today while you guys were with Brody. Said her name was Jill. She was looking for Ben, and she was dressed a little too provocative to be visiting a neighbor. That is just my opinion."

"Oh, she has always had a thing for Ben. She is a horrible flirt. I guess now that I am dead, she thinks it's a good time to make her move," Abby says, rolling her eyes.

"How do you feel about that? About Ben possibly moving on with someone else?" Hazel asks.

"What can I do about it? I think he will move on with someone else. He is not one to be alone. I do think he will have the decency to wait until I am really gone. I mean, I hope he does," Abby says.

"If he decides to move on this quick, he is going to get a swift kick in the balls from me. You're welcome," Hazel says, smiling.

Hazel has always been Abby's savior.

"Us against the world, right, Haz?" Abby says.

"Forever," Hazel says.

"Mom!" Brody screams.

Abby and Hazel run into Brody's room.

"What's going on, Brods? What's wrong?" Hazel says.

Abby sits by him on the bed and touches his hand.

"I hurt so bad, and I can't stop throwing up. It's just too much. I can't do this anymore," Brody says.

"Ben went to pick up the other medicine, but, Abbs, I don't think he can keep down any pills. I am going to call the doctor and see if they will give him higher doses of patches. Until then, let's change the patches and put two of the nausea on and two of the pain patches. Brody, do you have any weed? That will help you with nausea and pain," Hazel says.

"No, Aunt Hazel. I have been clean for a while now," Brody says as he gets up to go throw up.

"Abby, we need to get him some weed. Let me go call the doctor, and then I will go to the med store and pick up some weed for him," Hazel says.

"Haz, he has been clean for so long. We can't do that."

"Abby, I don't think it matters right now. Let's tackle one thing at a time, and he can't heal when he is fighting all of this pain," Hazel says.

Brody lies back down, and Abby starts to rub his head. He closes his eyes, and tears stream down his face. Abby hates seeing him like this. Why does he have to go through all of this? He just beat addiction and has his life together. Why in the hell is this happening? Abby is so mad she could hurt someone. God, why? What could possibility be the reason to subject someone to this?

"I called the doctor, and he is calling in stronger patches and says I can double up the ones we have now," Hazel says.

Hazel takes off the old patches and puts on the new ones, two each.

"I am going to the med store to pick up some weed. What matters now, Brody, is you. I am not saying you have to use it, but it will be here if you need it. That's all. I will be back shortly," Hazel says, leaving.

Abby continues to sit by him and rub his head. Even though he can't hear her, she sings. She sings all the songs he used to love when he was little. He seems to be relaxing a little more.

"Thanks, Mom. I love you," Brody says.

She leans over and kisses his head. Brody smiles.

Ben and Abby are sitting out back, letting the sun soak through their skin.

"Ben, this is the worst thing ever. It is not fair that this is happening to him. I don't understand it," Abby says.

"Abbs, it's not for you to understand. Things just happen, and most of the time, it's to good people. You have always had a strong faith. Don't give up on that now. God always uses bad things for good. There is a reason you are still here, Abbs, and that reason is Brody. You are keeping him strong," Ben says.

"Can I ask you something?" Abby says.

"Anything. What's up?"

"Hazel said Jill was here looking for you and was dressed a little too sexy for a neighbor checking in. I guess it is not really a question. It's more of a statement, but I want you to know I understand if you decide to be in another relationship after I am no longer here. I know you don't like being alone, and it would be nice to have someone to do life with. I get it, and I want that for you," Abby says.

"Abbs, I can't help that Jill came over here and that she was wearing whatever she was wearing. It has not even crossed my mind to have another relationship with anyone. I am actually good with being alone, believe it or not. I will be fine, but on the off chance I do get in a relationship with someone, they could never take your place. I will love you until the last breath I take. You are my girl," he says, kissing her lips.

"You always were a charmer. I love you," she says.

"Back at ya, babe," he says.

Abby goes to check on Brody, and he is sleeping. She sits on his bed and just stares at him.

"God, why am I still here? What do you want from me? It is not enough that I died. Now, I have to watch my baby go through yet another struggle of life and death. Why? No, really, I want to know why, God. Tell me. Now!" Abby screams.

Tears stream down her face. She just wants to know what to do. How can she make all this better? When you become a mother, your job is to protect your child from harm. Abby holds on to the guilt of Brody's addiction for years, blaming herself that he is in that deep pit. If she would have disciplined him more, loved him better, the list is long for Abby.

She beats herself up for years. It takes her a long time to realize that his addiction issues are not a reflection on her. He makes choices, and all choices have consequences, either good or bad. She is so proud when he makes it to his one year clean and sober. Her heart nearly explodes with pride He has worked so hard to accomplish that milestone. Anyone who has those issues knows that it never goes away. It is always one day at a time.

"Ugh, kiddo, I love you so much. Hang in there. You can get through this. We will get through this together," Abby says as she leans over to kiss his cheek.

"We have all of his meds up to date. The new patches for nausea and pain. Also, I went to get some weed at the med store. Don't roll your eyes, Ben. If it helps him get through this, that is all that matters," Hazel says.

"No, I know you're right, Hazel. I just worry about his addiction," Ben says.

"One thing at a time, Ben. Even Brody is worried about that, but there is no way he could get through this without pain meds. No way. So let's not bring this topic up to him. He is his own worst enemy. Trust me, he is beating himself up enough about this," Abby says.

Hazel can see that Abby is going into mama bear mode. She also knows that Abby has had to fight many people over Brody's addiction. Everyone always has opinions on what she should do and how she should do it. Abby just loves her kids so much and always wants good things for them. Hazel loves her for it.

Brody goes looking for his family. He swears he's been asleep for days. For the first time in a long time, he feels like he could eat something. He looks out the window of the kitchen and sees Hazel talking. No doubt talking to Abby. This whole thing with Abby still feels like a dream to him. God has a real sense of humor, that's for sure. Brody shakes his head and grabs a water out of the fridge and heads outside with Bogo right on his heels.

"Well, I think I may have broken the record for sleeping the most," Brody says, sitting down.

"Well, you needed it. That's for sure. How about something to eat? Do you think you are up for that?" Hazel says.

"Actually, yes. Maybe some soup or something?" he says.

"Okay, consider it done, and I will make you a shake. You need some protein. Be back in a flash. Oh, and your mom is right next to you if you want to chat," Hazel says.

With that, Hazel is off to make some soup. Abby gives his hand a squeeze.

"Mom, what a mess, huh? I mean, if I didn't have bad luck, I wouldn't have any. What is crazy is I don't crave all this pain medicine. I don't feel crazy like I have to have it. It seems different this time. I can't really explain it. I have always felt so at ease talking to you, Mom. You have never judged me. You always made me feel loved even when I was totally unlovable. Thank you for that. Thank you for being the best mom ever," Brody says.

Abby hugs him tight, never wanting to let go.

"Soup is ready. Come on in and eat. It is getting a little chilly out there," Hazel calls out.

He and Abby head into the house. Brody tries to eat as much as he can. His stomach feels like it's in knots, so he stops while he's ahead.

"Thanks, Aunt Hazel, for making the soup. While I still have a little energy left, I am going to hit the shower and get back to bed," Brody says, getting up.

"I will change your patches when you are out of the shower. I will be in there as soon as I clean up in here," Hazel says.

"You have done plenty. I will do the cleaning, Haz," Ben says, finishing up his soup.

"Perfect. I will go call John and the kids," Hazel says.

"Well, Brods ate more than I thought he would. I suppose there will be good days and bad days. I just wish none of this had to happen. I would give anything for our old lives. I miss our life," Abby says sadly.

Ben gives her a hug and kisses her forehead.

"I know you do, Abbs, but this is bigger than any of us. God is in control, and our job is to trust the process no matter what we think is best. I will tell you one thing. Brody is a strong man. He can get through anything and that I am sure of," Ben says as he cleans up the kitchen.

"You always say the right things, Ben. How do you do that?" Abby asks.

"It's a gift, Abbs."

He laughs. She gives him a push, laughing with him.

The Scan

BRODY WALKS IN the kitchen, looking for his family. They are all there sitting at the bar.

"Well, I just got a call from the doctor's office. They want me to come in tomorrow morning to go over the scan in person. She said they would have it on the screen when they go over it, and it would make more sense. So that sounds real good," he says sadly.

Abby goes over and hugs him. He smiles.

"Brods, let's keep positive," Hazel says.

"I called Megs already. She asked me to call as soon as I found out anything. She is coming with us to the appointment in the morning. I told her she didn't have to, but you know Megs," Brody says.

"We will all go, and I don't want to hear anything about it," Hazel says.

"Let's all try not to focus on this tonight," Abby says.

"I agree, Abbs. Brody, are you ready to try some soup? Shake?" Hazel asks.

"Actually, these new patches are working pretty well. For the first time in a while, I don't feel pain. So yes, I will try some soup and a shake," he says.

"Remember the time Brody got twelve stitches in his knee? He was feeling better so he thought he could take the stitches out. He literally took all of the stitches out, and we had to take him back to the hospital to get more put in. That's my Brody," Ben says, laughing.

They all laugh. Abby is thinking how good it is to see her family laughing in the midst of all the tragedy they have been through. It makes her heart so happy.

"Oh, I almost forgot to tell you guys. I got an email, and my medical leave is approved. That's a load off my mind. I have worked so hard for that job. They have promised me that my job is there when all of this shit is over," Brody says.

"That's great news! You definitely did not need that worry right now. Your main thing to deal with is getting back to your healthy self. That's all you need to focus on," Hazel says.

Brody has had to keep his phone on silent. It never stops ringing. All of his friends have been concerned about him. There is one person he has stayed in contact with, and that's Emma. He hasn't told a soul, but he has had his eye on her for a long time. They have gotten close in the last year. She thinks they are just friends, and they are, but he wants so much more with her. He is going to tell her that until his life got derailed with the cancer. If he makes it through this, he vows to tell her first thing. For now, they talk and text every day. She has been a huge help in keeping his mind clear and focused on recovery.

"Earth to Brody," Hazel says.

Laughing, Brody looks at her. "Sorry, Aunt Hazel. What's up?" he says.

"I was asking you if you wanted to play a board game or watch a movie?" she says.

"I am going to give you a hard pass on the board game. I will try to stay awake for the movie," he says.

"Okay, let me get your patches changed, and we will find us a good one," she says.

"Actually, there is someone I need to call. Could we do a movie another night?" Brody says.

"Of course, but let's go and get the patches changed. I need to call John anyway," Hazel says.

That leaves Ben and Abby.

"You look like someone has beat you up, Abbs. Spill it," Ben says.

"I don't have a good feeling about this Ben. If it were good news, they would have just told him on the phone. I mean hasn't he been through enough? I go through being at peace with things to being mad as hell. I just wish there was more I could do. I feel so helpless," she says.

"Abby, you are still here for a reason. Use this time to talk to God. I'm betting your prayers are ones he is really listening to these days. After all, you are dead but still here. As someone on the outside looking in, I see you helping Brody more than you think you are. You give him a peace and a comfort that none of us can," Ben says, hugging Abby.

"Thank you," she says, leaning into his arms.

It is late, and they are all sleeping. Abby just goes from room to room, watching her family that she loves so much. She knows now that they will be fine when she leaves this earth. They are a strong bunch. Sitting on the edge of Brody's bed, she looks at him, and he seems so peaceful that it is hard to believe he is so sick. She prays, prays for his recovery, prays for journey to Heaven, and prays for her family to be healed from all of the pain they have been through in this past year. She knows in her heart that whatever happens, this family will be okay. She kisses her baby on the forehead. It seems like yesterday that she held him in her arms for the first time. He and Megan are the best things that ever happened to her. She is grateful for the opportunity to have been their mom. Bogo looks at her.

"Thank you for being his best friend. You have been a good dog," Abby says to him, and he reaches his head to her giving her a big sloppy kiss. She laughs.

"Of course, you can see me. Why wouldn't you, right?" she says, petting his head.

The next morning, Abby is in the kitchen when Ben walks in.

"Well, you are a sight for sore eyes. Good morning, beautiful," he says, giving her a kiss.

"Good morning, handsome. How did you sleep?" she says.

"I actually slept through the night. Usually, I wake up a million times, but last night was peaceful," he says.

"Good. You needed that. You aren't going to believe this, but the dogs can see me," she says.

"Abbs, there is nothing I wouldn't believe at this point. It is something crazy and new every day," he says.

"Good morning all. Coffee is needed and needed very much," Megan says, walking in.

"Good morning, sweetie. Coffee it is," Ben says.

Abby reaches out and gives her a quick hug.

"Hi, Mom. Love your hugs and is much needed this morning. The kids were up all night. I swear they took turns in waking up last night. It was bizarre, and of course, they wanted just me and not Cam," Megan says.

"Good morning, folks. Are we all ready for what today holds?" Hazel says, walking in.

"Well, I have never prayed so hard for anything in my life," Megan says.

"You and me both, sweetheart," Hazel says, giving her a hug.

"Well, today is the day. I wish they would have just told me the outcome on the phone," Brody says, grabbing a drink out of the fridge.

"That wouldn't be near as exciting, Brody," Ben says.

Abby walks over to give him a quick hug.

"Hey, Mom," he says.

They are all waiting in silence in the doctor's office. Each one of them is praying that the outcome will not be what they are expecting.

"Good morning to you all," Dr. Masters says, walking into his office.

They all say good morning in unison. He talks with Brody for a minute, asking him how he is feeling and if there are any new symptoms for him to be aware of.

"Okay, let's get to it," he says, pulling up the scans on a screen where they can all see.

Pointing to an area of the scan, he tells them that where they operated, there has been no new growth.

"Right here is what is concerning," he says, pointing to another area. "There seems to be a whole new growth right here. The image shows this particular growth is attaching itself to fibers in the brain that would be impossible to get to without causing a significant amount of brain damage. What I am trying to say is this seems to be aggressive, and surgery will not be possible this time. We will continue to treat with radiation and chemotherapy. We will go at it very aggressively, and we should know if that is working in a couple of months. Look, I know this doesn't look good, and I know this treatment will be devastating, but it is our only option," he says.

Brody sits there in shock. He can't even get the words out.

"Will this work, or will he be basically killing himself with the treatment?" Megan asks.

"I am not going to lie to you. This treatment will be brutal. It is the only chance we have," Dr. Masters says.

"And if he doesn't do the treatment?" Hazel asks.

"As aggressive as this seems to be, I would estimate three to six months of life left. I am sorry, Brody. I wish I had better news for you," he says.

Abby cannot stop the tears from streaming down her face. Again, she is grateful the kids cannot see her.

"Take a few days to think about what you want to do here, Brody, and if you decide on the treatment, we will start it immediately," Dr. Masters says.

Handing Brody all of the information to read on the treatments, they all get up to leave.

"If you have any questions or concerns, please call me. I am sorry, Brody," he says.

Getting home, they are all silent. Nobody has the words to make it all right.

"Hey, thanks for going, guys. I am going to lay down for a while," Brody says, leaving them standing in the kitchen.

They all go to sit outside, hoping the sun will make everything right. Megan is crying so hard she can't breathe.

"I can't lose him too. I can't. Why is this happening? My mom, now my brother. I am sorry to say this, but I am so fucking pissed off at God right now. There is not a good reason for this to be happening to our family. We are good people. This is absolute fucking bullshit!" Megan screams.

"It is bullshit. You are right, kiddo. There is not a reason in the world for this. I have no wise words for you. I am just as pissed as you are," Hazel says, holding her hand.

Abby walks over and sits by Megan and just holds her. They both cry like babies.

"Mom, why is this happening? I don't understand. I don't know what to do. I feel so lost," Megan says.

All Abby can do is hold her. She wants to make all this go away. But how? How is she going to do this? They all sit outside for what seems like hours going over the information the doctor gives Brody. The treatment sounds brutal, and will he survive that? Nobody has any answers.

Brody comes out after a couple of hours. He is showered and looks like he is leaving.

"Where are you heading, Brody?" Megan asks.

"I can't just sit here and wait to die. I am going out with a friend. Her name is Emma, and she is picking me up since I can't drive with the meds. Don't worry about me. I will be fine. I really just need to feel normal if only for a while. Love you guys. Don't wait up," Brody says, leaving.

"What just happened? Who is Emma? These are all good questions that I have," Megan says, laughing.

"I don't know, but it was good to see him happy for a minute," Hazel says.

"Well, I have to go home to the family. Love you all, and see you tomorrow," Megan says.

"Well, that leaves the three of us. Haz, I will go make some dinner for us. You and Abby relax out here," Ben says, getting up to go inside.

"Sounds good, Ben. Thanks," Hazel says.

"What are you thinking, Abbs? You have been really quiet all day," Hazel asks.

"I want Brody to be okay. I feel like me being here isn't helping anyone. I just wished I knew what I was supposed to be doing," Abby says sadly.

"You do the best with what you have. You make him feel better just with your presence. You have made things better for Ben, Megan, and myself. With your accident, none of us got closure. It was like one day you were with us and the next you were gone. I personally feel like there has been closure. Will I miss you when I can't sit and talk to you like this? Hell yes, but you being here just for a while longer has saved my life. I'm betting you have saved all of us from what could have been," Hazel says.

"Brody hasn't mentioned anything about Emma. I wonder if this is someone special?" Abby says.

"He needs this distraction right now. He needs to feel normal, and I think this will do wonders for his spirit," Hazel says.

Ben comes out with a tray full of goodies.

"Here you go, Hazel. I made burgers, salad, and a cold beer. Well, I didn't make the beer, but you get where I am going with this," he says, laughing.

"Thanks, Ben. Looks great," she says as she takes a big bite of the burger.

After they have eaten, they all sit in silence, reflecting on the day.

"It's getting chilly out here. I am going in, and I will clean up the kitchen. You cooked, and I will clean up," Hazel says.

All the dogs are sitting by Abby. Bogo is on her lap. Hazel looks at her before she gets up.

"It's amazing the dogs can see you. This entire thing has been amazing. If anyone ever tells me they doubt there is a God, well I have a story for them," Hazel says, laughing.

"How would you feel about snuggling up on the couch with a good movie?" Ben says to Abby.

"Sounds good to me," Abby says as they head to the living room.

"I will join you guys shortly," Hazel says.

Later in the evening, Abby and Hazel sit talking about old times while Ben sleeps.

"He didn't watch much of the movie," Hazel says.

"I am not sure he has ever finished a movie since I have known him," Abby says, laughing.

Brody comes in later in the evening. Hazel and Abby are still up.

"Were you two waiting up for me?" Brody asks.

"Us? No, of course not," Hazel says, laughing.

"How was your night? Did you have a good time?" she asks.

"It was awesome. For just a while, I felt normal. Emma is really a good person. We have fun together," he says.

Abby gives his hand a squeeze. He looks over and smiles.

"I have made a decision. I will do the radiation treatment, but I am not doing the harsh course of chemo that he suggested. I don't want to go through all of that and feel like complete shit for months and then die. I want to live my life and feel as normal as I can until I die. I hope that you guys can respect and understand my decision," Brody says.

Hazel looks over at Abby, and she has tears streaming down her face.

"I understand totally. I just have to believe that God has him in the palm of his hands. I just don't believe that his life will end here. I won't believe that. I have total faith that he will overcome this. He has to," Abby says.

Hazel tells Brody what his mother says.

"Mom, I know this hurts you to see me go through this. I mean what I have put you through in my lifetime. You have had your fill of pain when it comes to me, and I am sorry. Whatever happens, I am glad that I have had this extra time with you. I may not be able to see you, but I know you are here, and that has helped more than you know. We will get through this," Brody says.

"Yes, we will. We are a strong family, and no matter what happens, we are here for you, sweetheart," Hazel says, hugging him.

"Now, tell me how has the pain been? You need to get those patches changed," she says.

"Actually, my head has not been hurting as much, thanks to the patches. I'm going to get a shower, and then I will put new ones on. I am so tired. I feel like I could sleep for days. Love you, both. Good night," he says.

Hazel looks at Abby, and she can see that Abby is hurting.

"Abbs, we don't know that this will be the end for him. Hang in there. Only God knows the outcome of this one," Hazel says, hugging her sister.

The next morning, Megan comes over, and Hazel tells her and Ben Brody's decision on not doing anymore chemo.

"I think he's making a rash decision and not really thinking this through. If I can be honest here, I think he is being totally selfish. I'm sorry to say that. I know this has been hard on him, but what about us? Do we matter? Are we not enough to fight for?" Megan says.

Ben doesn't say a word. He doesn't really know how to feel about it. He understands Brody and also understands Megan. This has been hard on everyone.

"I know this is hard to understand, but at the end of the day, we can't make the decision for him. He has to do what is best for him. I'm sorry, Megs. I know this is hard for you. I can respect that," Hazel says.

Megan walks away and goes to Brody's room. She sits on his bed, looking at him. He opens his eyes startled that she is there.

"What the hell, Megs. What's going on?" he says.

"I just got the news. You know, the news that you were just going to give up on living. This is not okay with me, Brody. Why would you decide this?" she says.

"Megan, I am doing what I think is best for me. I don't want to go through all of this torture and then die in the end anyway. That time would be wasted on me being in agony. I want to enjoy my life. I want to go back to work. I want to date Emma. I want to feel like my life is normal. I am sorry if you can't understand that. I am definitely not doing this to hurt you," he says.

Megan is crying.

"You and Mom can't leave me. What will I do without both of you? I just can't do this. I need you both here. I know Mom won't be here for long. I just counted on you being here, Brody. I seriously don't think I will make it without you," she says.

"Trust me, this is not how I wanted my life to go. I want to be here. Here for you and the kids. Mom has always told us that prayer is powerful. Well, I am trusting her on this. God knows we need each other, especially when Mom is gone. I have to trust that he has a better plan for me than I have for myself. You are the strongest person I know, Megs. Whatever happens, you will come out on top. You have the kids to be here for. I will fight like hell to be here. I have been doing so much research on this. There is a special diet to be on. There are herbs you can use. I am going to try all of this. I am not giving up. I just don't want to waste my time being so fucking sick that I want to die. You know?" he says.

"I know. I get it. I will help you research, and we will get you on the best foods and herbs that will kick this cancers ass. You're right, Brods. You have a good mindset, and I am behind you one hundred percent. I love you so freaking much. Please never forget it," she says, hugging him.

"Love you too, Megs. Now, get the fuck outta my room. I'm tired as hell," he says, laughing.

"Well?" Hazel asks when Megan walks back into the kitchen.

"Well, he seems to have it all together in his head. He knows what he wants and how to achieve that. All we can do is pray. I am going to do some research on the diet and some herbs," she says.

"You and your research," Abby says, laughing.

Hazel laughs and tells her what her mom says.

"I wonder where we got the excessive researching from mom?" Megan says.

"I almost forgot to tell you guys that John will be here this weekend. He is missing me pretty bad right now. I know I should just be home, but I can't do it, not while you are here, Abbs. I just can't," she says.

"Aunt Hazel, you need to do what is right for you, and if that is being here with Mom, then that's what you do. I, for one, love having you here," Megan says.

"I second that," Abby says, smiling at her sister.

"All this love this morning. It's getting a little too mushy for me. I need a guy around here. It will be good to spend time with John," Ben says.

Brody and Emma

BRODY IS BACK to work and has been continuing to stay with Ben and Abby. Somehow, it makes him feel better having everyone around. Spending time with Emma has been a highlight. She has always been a friend to him, but now he sees her in a different light—more than a friend. Getting to know her, he knows she has good values. She loves her parents and siblings. She loves God and goes to church regularly. Sometimes, he thinks his mom has something to do with him seeing Emma in a different light. Emma reminds him so much of his mom—the caring, loving, and good-natured part. Emma is a nurse and works crazy hours, but when she is off, they try and spend time together. They talk several times a day. She has become an important part of Brody's life. Tonight, she is coming over to his parents for dinner and will meet everyone including Megan and her family. John is still here, so there will be an array of family fun. He only wishes Emma could meet his mom. She would have loved Abby.

Abby and Ben are sitting outside, enjoying the sun. John and Hazel are at the store, getting everything they will need for dinner.

"I am excited to see Emma and Brody together and see how they interact with each other. He has never brought anyone here for us to meet," Abby says.

"She must be special to him. That's for sure. I think she has helped him feel a sense of normalcy through all of this," Ben says.

"You're right. I have noticed a major difference in his attitude. Do you think he made the right decision with stopping his treatment?" Abby asks.

"Only he could have made that decision, Abbs. He has to do what is right for himself. He goes for his scan next month, so we will know more then," Ben says.

"Ben, I feel like my time is coming to an end. I can feel myself pulling toward something. I don't want to leave you. I love you so much," Abby says sadly.

"I know. I can feel it too, Abbs. Something feels different, and I can't really explain it. We will be together again. You are my person, and there will never be anyone else. Why have anyone when you have already had the best? Right?" Ben says.

"Oh, you always were such the charmer," she says, kissing him.

Brody walks in the house, looking for everyone, and sees they are all outside. He goes in his room and lies down for a minute. He still has these damn headaches. He tries to put on a brave face, but some days, they are overwhelming. He has been getting rides to and from work just so he can continue to take his pain meds. He must have fallen asleep as he wakes up startled. Looking at the clock, he sees he is only asleep for a few minutes. He gets up and takes more pain meds. He changes into jeans and a T-shirt. He sees Ben in the kitchen. Before he says anything to him, he sees him bend over, grabbing his chest.

"Ben, are you okay?" he asks.

"Brody, um, yeah, I'm fine. I have been having some heartburn lately. I guess I need to watch what I eat," he says, laughing.

Brody isn't so sure that's the case. He makes a mental note to talk to his mom and Hazel later about it.

Ben and John are over at the grill, getting the meat ready to go on. Brody sits down with Hazel and Abby.

"I can't wait to meet Emma, Brods. I know if you think she is something special, we all will," Hazel says.

He knows his mom is right next to him. He can feel her holding his hand. He looks over at her.

"Mom, I know you will love her. She reminds me so much of you. She is kind, funny, and loves Bogo. So can't go wrong there. Anyway, I know I can't introduce her to you or even tell her about you still being here, but just knowing you will get to see her and get to know her, well, it is better than you not knowing her at all. I think she is the one, Mom. I have never felt this way about anyone, ever. I have known her for so long. It was all of a sudden that I saw her in a different light. God works in mysterious ways," Brody says.

Abby squeezes his hand.

"Brody, you have always been so cautious with you heart, and seeing you like this makes my heart so happy. I think you have definitely found the right one. I say that without even meeting her because of how happy you are. That happiness is love. Follow your heart on this, and you can't go wrong," Abby says.

Hazel tells him what his mom says. Brody smiles. He has always cared what his mother and sister thought about things. They are his everything. The three of them have been through so much in the past. They get through it all, and they do that together.

"Have either of you noticed anything about Ben lately? I was in the kitchen, and he was bent over holding his chest. He says it is heartburn, and I am not so sure I buy that," Brody says.

"We both have noticed him not feeling great. He has also told us it's heartburn. Abby got him to make an appointment with his doctor, but they couldn't get him in until the end of the month. That's a few weeks away. He says he's fine. We will just keep an eye on him. I swear this family is falling apart," Hazel says.

Megan and her family come in, and the kids were excited to see everyone. Abby loves to see the kids and watch them play. They are getting so big. Abby gives Megan a hug before everything gets crazy. Megan smiles and whispers, "Love you, Mom."

Brody walks outside, and Emma is with him.

"Everyone, I would like to introduce you to Emma. Emma, well, this is everyone," he says, laughing.

They all welcome Emma and get up to introduce themselves to her. Abby watches her family. She is so proud that this is her family and how kind and caring they are to one another. She watches Emma and Brody throughout the night, and she now knows that Brody loves this girl very much.

Later that night when everyone has gone home, Hazel and Abby are in the kitchen.

"Haz, it's time to give Brody my ring. Watching him with Emma tonight confirms what I already knew. He's in love with her," Abby says.

"Abbs, what if he doesn't make it? Are you sure you want to give him that ring?" Hazel asks.

"Yes, he, at the very least, deserves that experience whether he lives or not," Abby says with tears streaming down her face.

Hazel gives her sister a hug.

"Well, what are you waiting for? Let's go give it to him."

They knock on his bedroom door, and Bogo barks.

"Yeah, come in," Brody says.

Abby and Hazel walk in.

"Well, I think tonight went well. Emma is a real sweetie," Hazel says.

"She sure loved all of you. She seems to fit right in," Brody says.

"It's nice to see you happy, Brody. You deserve happiness in your life. Listen, your mom is here with me, and she wants me to give you something," Hazel says, reaching into her pocket.

"You know this was your mom's, and she wanted you to have it. She says this is the perfect time to give it to you," Hazel says, handing him the ring.

Brody reaches out and takes it. Looking at the ring, he starts to cry.

"Mom, this was yours. You love this ring," he says, crying.

Abby reaches out and grabs his hand.

"That ring represented so much love for me. Now, it's your turn to have that love in your life," Abby says.

Hazel tells him what she says.

"Thank you, Mom, and I can absolutely see Emma wearing this. She is the person I want to spend the rest of my life with however long or short that may be. She is the one," he says.

"We know. That is why Abbs wanted to give this to you tonight. We love you, kiddo," Hazel says.

Brody can't sleep. He tosses and turns with thoughts running through his head. He wants to live. He wants to be here for years to come. He has never wanted something so much in his life. For the first time ever, he prays. He prays for his life to be long and healthy. He prays for his salvation. He prays for his family. He knows he takes life for granted. He always thinks he is superman. Nothing will ever happen to him. God sure shows him who is boss, and he vows never to take things for granted again. He now knows each day is a gift.

Fading

ABBY SITS IN the kitchen, watching the birds outside. It is still early, and nobody is up yet. She loves this time of day. It is peaceful and quiet. The last few days, she can feel something different happening with herself. She feels at peace and tranquil. Things seem to be brighter and almost in a different dimension. It is strange to her but not scary. She knows in her heart she will not be there with her family much longer. It is getting close to goodbye.

"Coffee, must have coffee," Hazel says, walking into the kitchen.

"You're up early. How did you sleep?" Abby asks.

"I slept okay but got up with John. He had an early flight home," Hazel says.

"You know you don't have to stay here. Everyone seems to be doing okay," Abby says.

"I know, and I'm not staying for everyone else. I am staying for me. I can't leave if you are still here. I want to be with you while I can. I know that won't be much longer. I can see something different in you," Hazel says sadly.

"Me too. Something is definitely different. I thought I was still here for Brody, and if he is doing better, maybe my time is over here. I don't know. None of this has ever made sense to me," Abby says.

"Honey, he stopped his treatment. I'm not sure that he is better. He is not as sick, and that is because he's not getting treatment anymore. It will take a miracle for him to live through this without any treatment. I, for one, do believe in miracles, and only time will tell," she says.

"Well, he goes for another scan next week. We will know more then. Ben goes to the doctor at the end of the month. My mind goes in forty different directions on why I am here and who I am supposed to be helping," she says.

"Abbs, just go about each day as you always would. Why you are here will come to you. Maybe it's me. Maybe I need you. I don't really care to be here without you. I was in a downward spiral before I came here. Maybe I am the one who needed you," Hazel says.

Abby gives her sister a hug. She doesn't want to be without her either.

"You will be just fine when I leave. You have your family and my family to look after. They will keep you plenty busy," Abby says.

"Well, just know I won't like it without you, and nothing will be the same," Hazel says sadly.

"Duly noted," Abby says, laughing.

"Good morning, ladies," Ben says, walking into the kitchen.

"Good morning, sleepyhead. Did you sleep well?" Abby asks.

"I feel like I could sleep all day. I just don't have any energy. Maybe a strong cup of coffee will help," Ben says.

Hazel and Abby look at each other, each knowing something is definitely off with Ben.

"I think you should call the doctor and tell them you need to be seen earlier. If they can't do that, go to another doctor," Abby says.

"Abbs, I'm sure it's just life. Things are a little crazy around here lately in case you haven't noticed. It is all just catching up with me. That's all," Ben says.

Abby knows there is some truth to that, so she drops it.

The Good News

GETTING OUT OF the shower, Brody can hear his sister talking in the kitchen. He dresses and goes out to see what's up.

"Good morning," Brody says.

"Hey, Brods, any news yet?" Megan asks.

Brody had his scan yesterday, and everyone is anxious on the results.

"Not yet, but it is only seven thirty in the morning, Megs," he says.

"Well, I have been up since the crack of dawn, so it seems much later than that," she says, laughing.

"Since everyone is up and here, I have something to tell you. I am actually waiting on the scan results, and if it comes back good, I am going to ask Emma to marry me. I love her, and we all know that time is precious, and I don't want to wait anymore to start a life with her," Brody says.

"Wow, I guess I didn't know things were that serious for you two. That's exciting news. I am so happy for you Brody," Megan says.

"You have come along way, kiddo. I am excited for your future," Ben says.

Abby walks over and hugs him as tight as she can.

"Thanks, Mom. I love you," Brody says.

"This is the best news. I am so happy for you, Brody. You deserve all the happiness life has to offer," Hazel says.

"Well, I am off to work. Love you guys," Megan says.

"Yep, me too. I will call if I hear anything about the scan," Brody says.

Ben looks over at Abby, and he can tell something is different with her. She looks different, and he can't really put his finger on why.

"I can already tell you both that the scan will come out just fine. I can see it in his eyes. Brody is going to be okay. I can also feel something different in myself. It is like I am here, but something else is pulling at me. It's strange. I don't think I will be here much longer."

Ben and Hazel go over to hug her. They will miss her so much. Hazel starts to cry.

"I thought I would be ready for this, Abbs, but I guess you are never really ready to lose someone you love so much," Hazel says.

"I love you too, but, Haz, you will get through this, and I will be waiting for you," Abby says.

Ben, Abby, and Hazel are outside enjoying the afternoon sun when Brody walks out. He comes over and sits across from them.

"The doctor called with the scan results. The biggest tumor is completely gone. There is a small one that is still there, but it has shrunk with the radiation that I have still been doing. He thinks that with more radiation, I could be cancer-free. I went from dying to having my life back. I have never been so happy in my life."

Abby hugs him, and she is crying.

"Mom, I know this was because you are here. If you were not here, I would not have come through this. It is a true miracle. God has been so good to me," Brody says.

Hazel and Ben are now crying.

"This is the best news this family has had in a long while," Ben says, hugging him.

"I second that," Hazel says as she gets up to give him a hug.

"I called Megs on the way over here to tell her and, of course, called Emma. I am taking Emma out tonight to celebrate. Hopefully, we will have more to celebrate when the night is over," Brody says.

"You keep us updated on how that goes. She will be lucky to have you for a husband, Brody. You are a wonderful man," Hazel says.

"Thanks, Aunt Hazel. Love you guys. I have to get back to work. See you later tonight," Brody says.

"My prayers have been answered. I have never been more happy or relieved about anything ever before," Abby says.

"It is definitely the best news we have had. I am going to go and call John," Hazel says.

Ben just sits and holds Abby close. They both feel so relieved. Their kids are doing well. Everything is good.

The Last Day

THE WEEK IS about over, and Hazel has decided it is time to go home. She will be leaving tomorrow. She knows Abby and her family are going to be okay. Brody is back at his own house now and feeling good. Emma says yes, and they are now in the planning stage of their big day. They decide to get married New Year's Eve, which gives them six months to plan. Everybody seems so happy and content.

"I can always find you outside," Hazel says.

"You are up early," Abby says.

"Well, it is my last day here, and I wanted to get my time in with you. My plan is to just pretend you are on vacation, and I will see you soon," Hazel says.

"I think that is a great idea, Haz. I feel like everyone is in a good place right now, except Ben. He is laying down right now. He never takes naps during the day. I think he needs to get in to see his doctor sooner rather than later," Abby says.

"Let's talk to him when he wakes up and see if we can get that done. Do you want me to stay, Abbs?" Hazel asks.

"No, you have been here so long and have done so much already. I'm sure your family misses you like crazy," Abby says.

"Well, if Ben needs me to stay, I will. We will just wait and talk to him," Hazel says.

Hazel closes her eyes and lets the sun soak in her skin. She has always loved these kinds of days. The sun has always healed whatever is wrong. Abby just sits and watches her sister. The love they have for each other is definitely a one-of-a-kind love. They have always been there for each other no matter what. It has always been a good feeling knowing you had someone in your life that you can count on.

Ben walks outside and looks at Abby. She looks up and sees him. He looks different, brighter maybe. She feels peace just looking at him. He reaches out his hand to her and smiles. She grabs his hand and stands up. She knows they are going somewhere beautiful and peaceful. She doesn't look back at her sister or her house. She only looks forward, just the two of them, together forever just like they have wanted.

The family holds a celebration of life for Ben. He died in his sleep that day. The coroner said it was cardiac arrest. Some say Abby stays to help Brody get through his illness. Others say it is to bring Ben home with her. They all know they are together, and that has brought them peace and comfort.

Epilogue

"THE WEDDING WAS beautiful. I know Abby and Ben are watching and loving every second of this. I am so proud of the both of you. You have handled everything with grace," Hazel says to Brody and Megan.

"I feel like Mom and Ben were here today. It just felt right, you know?" Brody says.

"Yes, I do know. I love you, Little Brother. We got this," Megan says, giving her brother a hug.

That night after the wedding, Megan is sitting in her home office going over some neglected paperwork. This whole wedding thing gets her a little behind. It is worth every effort she gives. It turns out beautiful, and her brother could not have been happier. She opens a drawer looking for her pen, and she sees it, the letter her mother had wrote to her. She never reads it. She remembers putting it in the drawer. She opens it to read with her hands shaking.

> My sweet Megan,
>
> If you are reading this, chances are I am no longer with you. Otherwise, you wouldn't have access to this letter. I want to start out by saying thank-you. Thank you for being more than I could have ever dreamed of. You, my dear, are my little spit fire. I have always admired your sense to tell someone what was on your mind. I love that about you. Now granted, we have butted heads a time or two because of it, but please do not lose

that quality. Always let people know where you stand. You have made me so proud to be your momma. You are strong, caring, and kind, and you have a wonderful wicked sense of humor. Your little laugh that you have when your nose scrunches up, it is precious to me. Now, let's get into the momma you have become. Wow! My grandbabies are the luckiest kids on the planet to have you for their mom. Live each day to the fullest. Even on your bad days when you lay your head on your pillow, always remember how blessed you are. You have worked hard since you were old enough to work, and, girl, I am proud of that. I could go on and on about how proud I am and why. Just know that I will be waiting for you up here in Heaven and know that I have picked out the best place for all of us to be together. Enjoy each day because they fly by! Remember bad times don't last, and you can always talk to me. Always. I will be listening. I love you to the moon and back, sweet girl. Until I see you again.

Your momma

Megan has tears streaming down her face. She misses her mother every day.

"I love you too, Momma," she says out loud.

She texts Brody to see if he has read his letter. Chances are he forgets all about too. He is leaving for his honeymoon in two days, and if he has time, he should read it.

Brody looks down at his phone and sees his text from Megan. He does forget. As he is packing, he looks for the letter. He opens the drawer by his bed, and there it is. His heart skips a beat. He picks it up, and opening it, he smiles.

CROSSOVER

My sweet Brody,

    Well where do I start? Chances are if you are reading this, I am no longer with you. I need you to know that I am so proud of who you are. You have been through hell and back and came out on top. I am in awe at how you have overcome your struggles with addiction. You have only wonderful things in store for you. You have a heart the size of Texas. You are caring, kind, and someone that your family can count on to be there. I love your dry sense of humor. Most people have no idea that you are funny, but I do and we always had laughs together. Your favorite thing in life seems to be pulling a good prank on somebody, and your dimples will shine. Don't ever lose sight of laughter. It will help you through anything. I love your fierce spirit when it comes to your family. You would never let anything happen to any of us. You have such a protective nature to you. Please always watch out for your sister and the kids. You may be the little brother, but you have always watched out for her. I know you have thought of yourself as a failure, but you have to know that I think you can accomplish anything you put your mind to. You are smart, witty, athletic, and, not to mention, handsome! Go out there, and make your mark in this world. This world needs you. I will always be with you. If you ever need me, I will still be there listening. For now, I must go, but I will be waiting for you in Heaven and will have a kick-ass home ready for you. Enjoy your life to the fullest as it goes by so fast. I love you, kiddo, to the moon and back.

Your momma

Brody just sits there for a minute, thinking about his mom. He will miss her every day, no doubt, but he knows her spirit lives on in both him and his sister. He picks up the phone to call Megan.

"Hey, Brody, what's up?" Megan says.

"I just wanted to let you know I love you. That's all," he says.

"Well, I love you too. Always remember that we have each other. Now, go and have the best time on your honeymoon," Megan says.

"Thanks, Megs, and one more thing. We are expecting a little girl in four months. I never got to tell Mom," Brody says.

"I am sure she knows and is so happy for you. This is the best news ever! I should kick your butt for keeping this from me, but I am finally going to be an aunt!" Megan says.

"I will call you when we get there, Megs. Love you. Oh, and we are naming her Abby."

About the Author

MEL ANDREWS WAS born on November 23, 1972, in Buffalo, New York. She now lives in West Des Moines, Iowa, with her husband. She has two adult children and three grandchildren. After writing several children's books, *Crossover* is her first novel with more to come.

CPSIA information can be obtained
at www.ICGtesting.com
Printed in the USA
LVHW110406090321
680957LV00007B/188